Heaven and Hell
and the
Megas Factor

ROBERT NATHAN

Heaven and Hell and the Megas Factor

DELACORTE PRESS / NEW YORK

Manufactured in the United States of America

First printing

Designed by Barbara Liman Cohen

Library of Congress Cataloging in Publication Data

Nathan, Robert, 1894–
    Heaven and Hell and the Megas factor.

    I. Title.
PZ3.N195He   [PS3527.A74]   813'.5'4   75-4820
ISBN 0-440-04328-X

ACKNOWLEDGMENTS

I have several people to thank for their aid and comfort in the face of my own feeble scholarship: my good and patient friends John Weaver, Thomas MacDowall, and Miss Lynn Roberts, and whoever it is who puts together the terrifying little paragraphs on page 2 of the *Los Angeles Times*. And I beg forgiveness of those other friends of mine who will find themselves (I hope to their amusement) in this book, accomplishing things—to say the least—a little beyond their usual.

For there be seas of blood within our bodies each according to its nature; that of the heart being bright while that of the bile or liver being of a darker hue, yet each contributing to the whole or company which does afford the body its virtue.

Too, the sun and the rain, the wind and the snow together form a weather, the loss of any providing a universal disaster. Therefore it is needful to know that opposites are necessary one to the other, both day and night, the Universe being half light and half dark, and neither can prevail, yet both together in just mixture do create an order.

Bernard de Treves, 1490 A.D.

Prologue

THE LAST great battle was being fought: Armageddon had arrived, as prophesied. But not in Esdraelon, or in the Valley of Jezreel, but in the air and in the firmament above the air, where the Hosts of the Lord, dejected and dissatisfied, fled in confusion through the winds of space, crying Eli, Eli, and looking for Michael.

"This is not at all according to Revelations," exclaimed the Seraph Azrael, dodging an arrow loosed against him by Belial, one of Lucifer's lieutenants.

He was right: madness rode the heavens, putting all to rout. The very forms of creation, based upon order, symmetry, and harmony, toppled and teetered among the stars, while disorder, in the persons of Apollyon, Beelzebub, Sathariel, the Dukes of Esau, Astaroth, Asmodeus, Belphegor, Adramalek, and Lilith, flashed like lightning across the firmament. Gabriel's trumpet suffered a solid dent, and the angel Raphael, who had befriended Tobias on the banks of the Tigris by rescuing him from a sea serpent, received a painful box on the ear from Moloch.

"Was it for this," complained Saint Boniface, managing to keep just one step ahead of a pitchfork in the hands of a follower of the Dukes of Esau, "that I blasted the giant oak of Thor and converted twelve hundred Teutons on the summit of Mount Gudenberg?"

Withdrawn behind a cloud, the three archangels, Raphael, Gabriel, and Michael, commander of the Hosts, watched with dismay the rout of their forces. "I do not understand this at all," said Michael.

Gabriel shook his head solemnly. "What we are seeing," he said, "is the result of what is happening elsewhere. While we have been celebrating the Church Triumphant up here among the clouds, our ancient enemy has discovered some new form of madness down there, among mankind; and thus inspired, is proving irresistible."

"Quite," said Michael.

"I suppose," said Raphael hesitantly, "one should really send someone down, to find out what's going on."

"You'll have to count me out on that one," said Michael firmly. "I've been there before.

"The Garden, and all that," he explained.

"Me too," said Gabriel. "I rather expect I'll be needed here with my trumpet."

"What does God say?" asked Raphael.

Michael shrugged helplessly. "Nothing," he declared.

All three archangels ducked as a fiery bolt flew over their heads. "*Merde,*" said Raphael, speaking in tongues.

Meanwhile, on earth, in the United States of America, Memorial Day was being celebrated with bands, parades, the sound of taps on thousands of bugles, the placing of wreaths on millions of graves, and one hundred ninety-seven tornadoes which, touching down here and there from Alabama to Ohio, flattened thirty-five towns and villages, devastated four hundred thousand acres of farmland, killed and maimed countless men, women, and children, and left the survivors without telephones. The black cloud-funnels could be heard from afar off, roaring like demons across the land; and in the sound of that roaring were the names of all the afflictions known to man. All over the planet there were wars, bombings, riots, murders, kidnappings, muggings, assaults, rapes, face-slapping, and hair-pulling. And Lucifer, gazing down at all this, was appalled.

"Look here," he exclaimed to Beelzebub, "things have gotten out of hand!"

And shaking his head, the fallen archangel mused: "We shall be left with an empty planet; and man, on whose curiosity, obstinacy, and imagination I had been counting to uncover the secrets of creation, will no longer be available to us."

"That," agreed Beelzebub, aiming a dart at a small angel who was fleeing in the direction of the North Star, "would leave us with very little to do but to fly around. For a very long time." To which Belial added,

"Have you any idea how long it would take the insects

ROBERT NATHAN

to create a civilization capable of building an atomic re-
actor? Billions of years!"

"Exactly," said Beelzebub. "As usual, we have bitten
off more than we can chew."

"It's either man," said Belial, "or cockroaches."

"What would you advise?" asked Lucifer.

"If I were you," said Beelzebub, "I'd send someone
down to cool it. To put the brakes on, as it were."

Lucifer nodded his head. "You're right," he said. "At-
tend to it, please."

"*Zu Befehl*," said Beelzebub who also could speak in
tongues when he had a mind to.

Chapter
1

IT WAS ONE of those lovely spring evenings in New York, gentle and a little sad. The air was still warm, but soft as though from use, the sounds slower. The brown and gray apartment houses past which the young woman was making her way toward the park were settled into a kind of weariness, somber and shadowy. She was alone in the street, a slender, old-fashioned figure in her long, full skirt, her lacy blouse with its puffed sleeves, and a straw hat adorned with a wide blue ribbon, under which her golden hair escaped in unruly curls. Her name was Sophia, and she was from out of town.

Luis, the doorman at the Mannewitz Arms Apartments on West 84 Street, stared after her with a faintly puzzled expression. It had been a dull day, and he had another two hours to go before quitting time. Nothing had occurred worth remembering; so he didn't know why he should suddenly think of his childhood in San Juan, Puerto Rico.

Later that night as he prepared for bed in his small cold-water flat on 118 Street, he said to his wife, for no particular reason,

"Not that I had what you might call an enjoyable childhood. But on the whole, I was happy, I think. More than what I am now."

"We went to church a lot," said his wife, a thin, weary woman who worked in a laundry on 125 Street.

"That, I know," said Luis. "It is of no relevance."

On her way to the park, Sophia passed Temple Sinai-Bethel where the rabbi, Dr. Simon Newhouse, was conducting the Sabbath service. The temple was by no means full; in fact, the gathering was sparse; but for a moment Dr. Newhouse, who had been preparing to read the Tenth Psalm ("Why standeth thou afar off, Lord? Why hidest thou thyself in times of trouble?"), felt that he was speaking to a multitude, and exclaimed instead,

"Oh, come, let us sing unto the Lord, let us make a joyful noise to the rock of our salvation!"

The members of the Sinai-Bethel (Reformed) congregation gazed at one another uncertainly. Were things, perhaps, not as bad as they appeared? Did the rabbi know something?

Dr. Newhouse announced the programs for the following week. "The Ladies Auxiliary will meet on Tuesday next at the house of Mrs. Leo Richards. The committee for the construction of a fountain on the campus of the Hebrew University at Givat Ram will meet at eleven A.M. on Wednesday at the house of Mr. Simon Robbins; a light lunch will be provided."

He felt weary; of what use was a fountain at Givat Ram? His wife had been molested on West End Avenue, almost in front of their apartment house.

Sophia continued on her way to Central Park. Her gaze was gentle and candid, her complexion clear. She entered the park at 85 Street, on the West Side.

Chapter
2

BUCKTHORNE walked up Broadway, past the cinema palaces, past the discount stores, the gay bars, the pornographic bookshops and magazine stands. Everywhere billboards and neon signs advertised the life around him, filled as it was with lust, violence, greed, and despair.

Whores of both sexes passed him on their sad, hurried, private errands; they gave him bold or furtive glances, but not for long. He was not unattractive, but there was something about his face which did not encourage familiarity.

A young man, of no exact age, conventionally dressed, he could have been taken for a New Yorker; but in fact, he was not, he was a stranger in town. His dark, inquisitive glance took in everything, missed nothing. The city surprised him, not only by its bustle and noise, but by its odor which was like a sour gas. He could almost taste it; it seemed like an effluvium.

It was early evening; the air was still, the street lights not yet turned on. It was the hour when the tide of life flows more slowly; yet the home-going crowds pushed past him in haste. There were no happy or eager faces; each face was closed, secretive, and joyless.

In turn, each passerby, on encountering Buckthorne, felt more irritable than before, less satisfied with himself, and more envious of those who had it better in the world. It was only a passing feeling, which lasted for no more than a moment or two: the middle-aged businessman, hurrying toward the subway entrance which would take him to Penn Station and his waiting family in South Orange, slowed his steps for a moment, wondering where he was going; and the young man on his way to meet his fiancée at the corner of 50th and Broadway had a sudden disturbing vision of Marilyn Monroe. There was no way to connect such sudden momentary disturbances with Buckthorne, for there was nothing unusual about his appearance, except for one thing: he appeared confident and composed.

Having crossed Columbus Circle, he turned east on Central Park South and entered the park at the Avenue of the Americas.

Chapter

3

LOOKING back from the far end of the Sheep Meadow, the great apartment houses and hotels along the southern edge of the park rose into the evening sky, distant, blue, and shadowy, and hung with lights like stars. Despite himself, Buckthorne felt a momentary admiration for earth's beauty: twilight was coming down softly, the air around him was already dim, and farther on, among the Rambles, shadows were deeper along the darkening paths.

It was at this point, just as he was entering these shadowy recesses, that he saw the girl and the three rough-looking young men who stood in her way. There was no doubt about their intentions, since one of them already had his hands upon her. For Buckthorne his duty, however disagreeable, was clear.

"Hoy!" he cried; "you there! Police!"

What happened next happened so fast that he could scarcely believe it. Suddenly the three hoodlums lay scattered in the bushes, and the young woman was flying through the air like a kite at the end of a leash attached to an enormous Great Dane which bounded past him in a rush of wind, bringing her thump against his chest; at which point she lost hold of the leash, her feet touched the ground, and raising one hand to rearrange her bonnet —a straw hat with a blue ribbon—she gave voice to a low, "Whew!"

Then, stepping back and recovering her balance, she extended her hand. "How do you do?" she said.

They shook hands gravely. "Are you all right?" he asked politely.

"Oh, yes," she replied; "quite. And thank you very much."

"For what?" asked Buckthorne in surprise. She made a helpless little gesture. "Why," she said uncertainly, "for whatever it was you did."

"I'm afraid I did very little," he said, "except call for the police. It was your dog who . . ."

"My dog?" She seemed confused for a moment. "Oh," she said finally; "yes . . . of course. Hugo."

"A very large animal," said Buckthorne. "He went past me, and disappeared. Should we go look for him?"

She shook her head. "No," she said, "let him be. He'll find me when he wants to. But thank you anyway."

And again she extended her hand. It was soft but firm, and her glance was friendly and unruffled. He saw the straw hat, the old-fashioned gown; she seemed to have stepped out of a more delicate time in history. He gave a slight bow.

"My name is Buckthorne," he said.

"And I'm Sophia."

There was an awkward moment before she withdrew her hand. "Well," she said at last, "it was very nice meeting you."

"Yes indeed," said Buckthorne. "Me too."

"Well . . ." she said.

"Well . . ."

"Well, good-bye."

"Good-bye."

He watched her as she walked away, seeming to melt into the blue evening air. Despite himself, he felt disturbed. Why should she remind him, like a sudden light fragrance, of the past? Indeed, what past? The past was a long time ago.

Sophia, too, was thoughtful. Buckthorne, she thought; Buckthorne. Did it matter? He was attractive, but also— perhaps—a little dangerous. His manner was correct; he had made no advances . . . yet there was certainly something about him . . .

Oh, well, she thought, I may never see him again. And in any case, I can always count on Hugo. She smiled, remembering how well the Great Dane had disposed of the hoodlums. "Good old Hugo," she said.

The Sheep Meadow was empty; so was the Mall and the path to the zoo. The whole park was empty and silent; she could hear, beyond that silence, the hiss and hum of the city, but the silence itself was disconcerting, even— considering what had happened in the Rambles—somewhat menacing. She decided to whistle a tune to herself, and chose "Abide With Me."

At the zoo farmyard, she stopped to pat the donkey's head. His patient, stolid warmth was a comfort to her, and helped to lift her spirits. There was no evil in a donkey; he had been man's friend and companion ever since Balaam. As for the donkey, he accepted her hand as he accepted everything else, in silence, as part of the mystery of life. A pat, a stick, a carrot, or an angel of the Lord—each came in its own time, out of the same unknown. But he had only spoken once, in Midian.

On Fifth Avenue, at 60 Street, the little hot-dog carts had already folded their umbrellas, and had gone home; but the old horse-drawn carriages still stood patiently along 59 Street, across from the fountain and the Plaza. How bright everything seemed, after the empty darkness of the park! The buses and taxicabs clattered by, filling the air with a surflike rumble. . . . What a beautiful city it was. She admired the lights, the tall buildings; and started down Fifth Avenue.

There were few pedestrians about, and those few she encountered seemed to eye her suspiciously, and to walk a little faster than before. Sophia was the only stroller, pausing now and then in front of the great shops to admire the glittering window displays, the golden jewelry, and the rich appointments.

She stood for a while opposite St. Patrick's Cathedral, staring up at its gray spires; how alike they were, these great cathedrals, remembrances of the past, monuments to man's immortal longings, witnesses to his triumphs, sanctuaries from defeat—but sanctuaries no longer. The great doors were closed; no lights shone out from the building whose broad steps gave back only the milky gleam of the pavement. Why, she thought impatiently, was the cathedral closed? Why weren't the doors open, and light and organ music pouring out? "Open up, Archbishop," she exclaimed, "and let us do some business!"

At this, a young woman in a very short, tight skirt approached her, swinging her shoulder bag. "Move on, sister," exclaimed the young woman; "this is my territory."

Sophia looked at her in surprise. "Your territory?" she asked. "I should have thought that it belonged to the Church."

"I don't care who it belongs to," said the young woman. "My name is Adelaide, and I'm the one who works it."

"In that case," said Sophia tartly, "in the Christian sense, I'd say you hadn't been working hard enough."

"I suppose you'd like to give me a few pointers," sneered Adelaide, swinging her bag.

"Certainly," said Sophia. "For one thing, you are not what I would call appropriately dressed."

"Never mind how I'm dressed," said Adelaide. "I pay my taxes. Just get your can the hell out of here."

"Don't be ridiculous," said Sophia. "I shall do nothing of the sort."

"All right," said Adelaide, "you've asked for it."

And she approached Sophia in a menacing manner. Sophia immediately took the stance of an Edwardian pugilist, such as she had seen in old prints at the Tate Gallery during the Huxley-Wilberforce debates. This posture, however advantageous to Mendoza, Cribb, Jem

Mace, and John L. Sullivan, did not deter Adelaide for a moment; she gave Sophia a sharp kick on the shin, followed by a karate blow which laid her flat on her back on the sidewalk.

At once she heard a low voice behind her remark, "You hadn't ought to have done that, Miss," and glancing back, she saw a policeman shaking his head sadly at her. Sophia sighed, and opened her eyes. "A bit late for that one, weren't you, Hugo?" she remarked; at which the policeman tipped his hat, replied meekly, "Yes, luv, I was," and walked quietly away.

What on earth? thought Adelaide. He didn't look like a New York policeman; he looked, she thought, rather like one of those London bobbies with the belt and the helmet. "What are you," she asked Sophia, "in vaudeville? You and him?"

Sophia sat up and rubbed her neck. "You know," she said accusingly, "that was a bit on the sneaky side, don't you think? I mean to say—kicking people on the shin?"

"Look, sister," said Adelaide, helping Sophia to her feet, "if I hurt you, I'm sorry. But I've got a living to make."

And as she brushed Sophia off, she added in a kindly voice,

"You look like a nice young kid. You could be in pictures, or something. You don't want to be on the streets."

"I assure you," said Sophia with what dignity she could muster, "in the sense of your meaning, I am not. Nor am I and my . . . my partner . . . in vaudeville. I am far from home, and simply trying to do . . . to do what I can . . ."

Adelaide shook her head sympathetically. "It's a hard life," she declared. And then, moved by a sudden feeling of compassion,

"Come on," she said. "Let me buy you a drink."

Seated at the bar of the Hotel Westbury on Madison Avenue, Adelaide held forth on the difficulties of life for a woman in her profession. "It's a new game," she said. "It used to be a man was married or not; he had to pay for what he got, one way or the other. So a girl like me knew what she was up against: either his wife or his solitude. Now he doesn't have to marry anyone, no signing on the dotted line, everything's free: shack up, move in, move out, without even a blood test. Girls aren't asking for a wedding ring anymore, or even a fur coat; just a place in the bed and their own toothbrush. And they're learning the tricks. It used to be we'd teach the young boys and console the old men; well, the old men, they've got their porno movies now, and the boys have got their girls right out of high school. What I mean is, nobody wants to be a virgin anymore. So where does that leave us pros?"

Sophia shook her head. "I really don't know," she said.

"Exactly," said Adelaide. "So what we need is a union. Like out in Oregon or Nevada or one of those Western states, the girls are organized; there's one town they've got the local madam running for mayor. We need to pass a few laws, like making marriage respectable again, and against adultery."

"You mean," said Sophia thoughtfully, "you'd like to go back to the old days?"

"They weren't so bad," said Adelaide. "At least a girl didn't have to learn karate to keep from getting mugged."

"Yes," said Sophia, "that's it. I was almost 'mugged'— is that the word?—in the park by three young fellows —little more than boys, really . . . young boys . . ."

Her voice trailed off; she saw in her mind the face of the stranger against whose breast she had rested for an instant . . . what was his name? Buck . . . Buck-something . . . Buckthorne? . . . and felt a curious shock, as though she had been suddenly arrested and embraced . . .

"Young boys," she said, forcing her voice back to its business again. "Such violence. And in the young!"

She turned earnestly to her companion. "Tell me," she said, "where does it all come from? How does it begin?"

Adelaide toyed thoughtfully with her glass. "Have you ever been to a big rock concert?" she asked.

Chapter
4

BUCKTHORNE continued on his way uptown through the park, skirting the Reservoir, and coming out at 110 Street and Seventh Avenue. He had a number of calls to make on the upper West Side before attending to more serious business downtown, and at each one he had the same message to deliver. Those he met treated him with respect, but it could be seen that his message surprised them. "You cry Peace," exclaimed the Reverend Isaac Jones, "where there is no peace." He took Buckthorne to be a traveling evangelist. And Idi Abu, born Henry Washington Carter, demanded,

"Shall we leave our country, our ripening fields of grain, and whatever, to the honky?"

He spoke from his headquarters in the basement of a tenement on 118 Street. At hand were several sticks of dynamite and a machine gun ready to be shipped to Ireland.

Buckthorne went to call upon a famous playwright in

an apartment on Central Park West. "Would it not be possible," he asked, "to bring a more conciliatory spirit into your next play?" To which the playwright replied,

"No way."

He went on to explain his position to the visitor whom he took to be a reporter from *The New York Times*. "It's like this," he said. "When I first started out, I was cool. I talked kind of low, and I got a few crumbs thrown my way. Nobody knew my name. But when I got hot, and shouted—man, they came running! They brought me whole meals. You got to tell them who you are; you got despair, you got to lay it on them."

Buckthorne sighed. He wished that he could finish his business, and get home again; he wished that he could forget the meeting with Sophia in the park, and the feeling he had experienced when she rested for a moment in his arms. Whatever it was, he couldn't remember having experienced anything quite like it, and it troubled him. It had been, after all, a rather amusing meeting, hadn't it? So why should there be a sense of sadness mixed up in it? Something left behind—an aftertaste, neither bitter nor sweet, but bittersweet. . . .

He was not used to complicated feelings; his had always been simple and direct. As far back as he could remember, he had obeyed commands, carried out orders. Had someone "laid a despair" on him? He smiled ruefully to himself.

But there was no time, now, for such thoughts and questions. He had work to do.

Hailing a cab, he gave the driver an address on the East

Side, and settled back in his seat to study the city. The cab was a compact, small and comparatively new, but already worn out; it rattled and bumped over the asphalt, through the 96 Street transverse, and down Fifth Avenue. How naked the pavements appeared under the city lamps, no one walked, there were no pedestrians either on the avenue, or in the side streets. He could sense fear, like a cloud, all around him and above him in the lighted, locked, and bolted apartments; and he nodded with satisfaction. Fear was something he understood very well; it was part of the business.

Even he, himself, had been afraid once, long ago . . . falling, one of a vanquished host, down through the heavens . . .

Sieg Heil!

Without meaning to—and unaware that the driver behind the glass partition could hear him—he had spoken aloud, though ironically. "So what is it?" asked the driver, whose name he now saw was Levitsky. "You a Nazi or something?"

"No indeed," said Buckthorne. "And I am sorry if I offended you.

"Though I did," he added, "fly with the Luftwaffe for a while."

Mr. Levitsky turned around and looked at him. He saw a young man obviously in his twenties or early thirties, who didn't look as if he had been born before the end of World War Two. "Yeah," he said. "Sure." And turning back to his driving again, he murmured under his breath,

"Son of a bitch."

"Thank you," said Buckthorne cheerfully. Mr. Levitsky's eyes popped open. So what's he thanking me for? he wondered.

The fact was that Buckhorne was in a cheerful mood. The whole city, as far as he could see, was in a state of decay, the streets in need of repair, the once elegant hotels and apartment houses grown shabby, and the citizens frightened. In a way, he was sorry: the elegance and affluence of the past had been good for business. However, there was a favorable side to everything, if one looked far enough: as one city declined, it opened up other vistas; if New York, as he could now see, had been oversold, how about Cincinnati, and Joplin, Mo.?

For after all, in a sense, and looked at in a certain way, he was a salesman, and far happier selling his line than calling it in.

The taxicab pulled up before a large apartment house fronting Fifth Avenue at the northeast corner of 71 Street, and Buckthorne, after tipping Mr. Levitsky the proper fifteen percent plus a dime, was carried up in a paneled elevator to the penthouse where several gentlemen awaited him. The apartment itself, furnished in excellent taste and with the finest antiques, was surrounded by a terrace on which were to be seen all manner of flowering bushes, exotic plants, and even trees set in huge wooden tubs. Walking out onto the terrace, Buckthorne stood, as it were, in a garden; while around him he could see other penthouses similarly planted, softly lighted under the blue night sky. They reminded him of something . . . what was it? . . . long ago. And then he remembered the hanging gardens of Babylon. They, too, had flowered for a while, in a city beside a river.

Far below him the buses grumbled their way along the bright, empty avenue, on whose far side stood the park, dark and deserted; and once again he thought of Sophia.

"Well, gentlemen," he said at last, turning back to the silent, waiting men inside, "you probably know why I am here."

"No," said a large, middle-aged, swarthy man who was evidently spokesman for the group. "We don't. Everything is going good. So what's to complain?"

"We are not complaining," said Buckthorne; "on the contrary."

"So then," asked the spokesman suspiciously, "what?"

Buckthorne took a deep breath, and sighed. "Everything is going too well," he said. "It is time to cut down."

"Cut down?" demanded a small, dark, nervous-looking man with a tiny moustache. "You crazy?" And another, a fat man with a large nose, exclaimed, "Things have never been so good."

"Nevertheless," said Buckthorne.

The spokesman rubbed his chin, looking uncertainly at his colleagues. "This is a strange thing," he said slowly. "How do we do this? We are into everything; into films, into books, hotels . . . into Washington itself. And into the record business: we have already half a dozen of the biggest rock groups. And now Turkey is growing poppies again."

"Just the same," said Buckthorne.

"Just the same what?" asked the fat man with the large nose.

"The Big Man said to cool it," said Buckthorne.

A glum silence descended on the group. "He does?" asked the small man at last, in a subdued voice.

"He does," said Buckthorne firmly.

The spokesman sighed. "I suppose," he said tentatively, "he has his reasons."

"He has," said Buckthorne. And he added a little plaintively, "Look: I'm no happier about this than you are. But orders are orders. You know that yourselves."

They all nodded solemnly. "We know that, all right," said the spokesman. "Only we don't understand it."

"You don't have to," said Buckthorne. "As a matter of fact," he added frankly, "neither do I. It has something to do with entomology."

"Entomology?" asked the fat man. "That has to do with what?"

"Insects," said Buckthorne. "Bugs."

Later that night, the spokesman made an intensive search of his apartment for concealed microphones, but found none.

And Buckthorne went on to other meetings.

One of these was a meeting with seven state legislators, a judge of the Criminal Courts, Sec. 3, and a monsignor of the Archdiocese of New York. They met in the small back room of Reilly's Restaurant and Bar on Second Avenue.

"It is of the utmost importance," Buckthorne told them, "that we bring back the death penalty, with no more than one appeal to be heard within two weeks of conviction, and the sentence of death, preferably by hanging, to be carried out no more than a week later."

And he showed the legislators and the priest a set of statistics drawn up by an actuary in Texas. "As you can see," he said, "of the 4346 murders committed along the Eastern seaboard during the past eight months, not counting family quarrels, 17.8 percent were committed by men already convicted of one or more murders, but let loose upon the streets either by reason of their being out on bail while awaiting sentencing, or on parole, or released from custody by the psychiatric facility to which they had been entrusted, or simply by reason of having had access to a knife or a gun while in prison, and with it killing another inmate, or a guard, or taking hostages and bargaining for freedom. Swift retribution at the end of a rope would have saved some 709.21 lives last year in the states of Massachusetts, Connecticut, New York, New Jersey, Pennsylvania, Washington, D.C., and Texas—lives among which several could have been counted upon to advance the cause of science, which is of such importance to my organization."

To this, the judge replied thoughtfully, "We seek rather to rehabilitate, than to punish. Death is too conclusive; from death there is no rehabilitation."

"Yet, as you can see," replied Buckthorne, pointing to the sheaf of papers, "the percentages are against you. Less than eleven percent go forth to sin no more."

The monsignor cleared his throat. "According to Matthew, 18:12," he observed, "if a man has a hundred sheep and one of them is gone astray, does he not leave the rest to seek that one which is gone astray?"

Buckthorne turned a trifle pale, but stood his ground. "Jesus was not an actuary," he said. "Besides," he went on quickly, "is it not better to receive the soul of a convicted murderer confessed, absolved, and shriven, all in a short space, than to watch it wither and shrivel with hate year after year for a long period, cursing God and mankind?"

"There's something to be said for that, Father," remarked Representative Weinberg from the Bronx.

"Of course, of course," murmured the priest. At the same time it crossed his mind that the Devil was also known to quote Scripture when it suited him; but the thought seemed inappropriate. After all, the Lord had said, "An eye for an eye"; on the other hand, He had also said, "Justice is mine." Death—by hanging or by any other means—was scarcely the concern of the Church; her concern was rather with the ingathering of souls.

"What is the name, again, of this organization you're lobbying for?" asked Senator Woczynski.

"Actually," said Buckthorne, "our people prefer to remain anonymous. However, you might say that they are interested in the future of man. The F.O.M."

His face took on a meaningful expression. "Gentlemen," he said solemnly, "I represent a very wealthy organization. Very, very wealthy indeed; and one that knows how to reward its friends."

Several legislators coughed and hummed, pursed their

lips, and studied their fingernails; the judge gazed fixedly at the table, while the monsignor fingered his rosary in a thoughtful way. The future of man? What other future was there for him, except in God's grace? Still, it was probably true that a man about to be hanged was more likely to turn to the Church for consolation, than one caged up for life.

"Ah, well," he said finally, "I see no reason to . . . I mean . . . I think that the Church would not oppose a bill to . . . that is, if such a bill were to be presented to the legislature . . ."

There was a general sigh of satisfaction and nodding of heads. And Buckthorne went on to other meetings.

Chapter

5

IN HIS tiny flat on West 47 Street, the old gentleman who had once been an accepted novelist laid down his pen and closed his journal on the cover of which his name was inscribed in faded gold letters: Michael George. He had just set down his thoughts for the day, which was all the writing he allowed himself. Yesterday, he had written, I was obliged to listen to the latest composition of my friend Aaron Aaron. I must confess, it was not very enjoyable. "Tell me," I asked him, "what is the difference between noise and dissonance?"

"Dissonance," he explained to me patiently, "is the result of ordered application of inharmonious sounds. Noise is sound without order, or the result of accident. For instance, the whine of a buzz saw and the screech of a trolley wheel, if placed together by design, create a dissonance; but if by accident, they create a noise."

My friend's suite for four bass instruments, a teakettle,

three steel bars, and a square of sandpaper had just been performed by the Cleveland Chamber Orchestra. "Actually," he went on, "there is no such thing as noise, there are only sounds. The ear responds to what it has grown used to. Or anyway," he added honestly, "what is left of the ear."

But even to him, art has its limits. He went on to describe a concert in which every member of the orchestra was asked to play whatever pleased him at the moment; and a piece for the piano in which the pianist was not allowed to touch the keys. "That is very amusing," he remarked, "but should it be called art?"

My father loved the music of Beethoven, Schumann, and Schubert, Brahms, Wagner—the great Romantics; he used to play symphonies and concertos on a pianola which he pedaled with his feet. As a boy I listened to Grieg, Dvořák, Mendelssohn, Chopin, Liszt; I was filled with dreams both happy and sad, but full of longing. Will some young, dreaming boy listen to my friend's teakettle in the future?

I suppose it is possible. But when I think about the future, I must admit that I cannot imagine it. Or even if there will be such a thing as a future. Will someone, thousands of years from now—some creature more or less human—discover these scribbled words, these curious scrawls, and find them as meaningless to him as a bee's walk is to me?

There is one difference at least between my father and myself: it never occurred to him that the world wouldn't go on as before, that Brahms would be forgotten, or that simple English prose would ever appear as indecipherable as bird-song.

My friend has promised to take me to a rock concert.

Michael George put his notebook away in the drawer of his desk, and taking down an old, faded overcoat and an ancient high hat, went out to his place of business at the south end of the park opposite the Plaza. There, shaded by a large umbrella, he occupied the coachman's seat on an aged victoria, and waited for passengers.

Buckthorne spoke to a group consisting of several members of the SLA, the Weathermen, and certain other organizations. "In spreading terror abroad," he told them, "you defeat your own purpose. Each time you shoot a policeman or bomb a building, you harden the heart of society against you."

"Society has no heart," said a young man whose long hair was tied in a pigtail behind his back. And a large black man exclaimed,

"Power to the people!"

"What, then, do you aim for?" demanded Buckthorne. "Revolution? It will not turn out to be what you expect —an anarchical Utopia, or even a Marxist commune; but, as in the case of every industrialized nation, and also in the case of the emerging nations of the Third World, it will be a military dictatorship."

"So what?" exclaimed a youth of eleven, wearing a kitchen knife stuck in his belt. He saw himself standing triumphantly over the bodies of his father and mother, his older brother, his Uncle Joe, and Jerry Karakas, aged twelve, who lived on the next block and owned a Honda.

"At least," said a girl of fourteen, fondling a subma-chine gun, "we'll get some of the pigs first."

Her father was a wealthy manufacturer. She had had a luxurious childhood, but now for the first time she was enjoying herself, and was already pregnant by the young man with the pigtail. "Oh, wow!" she said. "Bang, bang, bang. How do you like that, Daddy?"

Buckthorne left the meeting with a heavy heart; he was troubled, he felt that things were getting away from him. And the worst of it was that he saw only too clearly how his own past efforts and those of his associates had en-couraged those very actions that he was now being asked to restrain. " 'Accents of mine were in the fierce melee,' " he murmured ruefully, quoting an all-but-forgotten poet of the First World War, who had died in battle; if he had lived, he would have been an old man now, and a member of the Academy.

It was easy to do—and so hard to undo what had been done. It had been so easy to tempt Judas; thirty pieces of silver was all it took. What a mistake that had turned out to be! He thought of all they had had to go through since then: the defeats—Anthony, Augustine, Theresa, Francis, Gregory, Luther . . .

And now, when there had been no defeats for almost a generation, when it had seemed so easy—they had over-shot their mark again! And he, of all things, had been sent to set things right. "Why me?" he exclaimed, gazing angrily up at the heavens.

A cat hissed at him from the gutter, and a rat ran out of a grating at his feet. "Oh, all right," he said grumpily, and went on to a meeting with the vice-president in charge of programming at NBC.

The vice-president was not altogether sure who Buckthorne was, but he seemed familiar, and there was no mistaking his air of authority. Perhaps he was from the FCC.

"The reason," he said, "that there is so much crime and violence on the tube, is because that is what the public wants to see."

"And what age is that public?" asked Buckthorne.

The official remained calm: "Our advertisers do not count years," he explained. "They count bodies."

"There is too much violence," said Buckthorne. "The minds of the young are being turned from what should be their chief concern, which is to discover the secrets of the universe, so that we . . ."

He stopped himself abruptly. "We are not pleased," he said coldly.

"And when," he asked, "do you show the great love stories of the past?"

"Early in the morning," said the executive. "During breakfast."

Meanwhile, Sophia was addressing a group of ladies assembled in the parlor of Madame Berthe's House of Beauty. "In Heaven," she declared, "all is forgiven; all are equal before the Throne."

"Let me ask the sister," said a young woman who had

decided to change her style of life, and to run for Congress on a women's rights platform in the next election, "what are the names of the archangels?"

"Michael, Gabriel, and Raphael," said Sophia promptly.

"I notice," said the young woman quietly, "that these are the names of men. Are there no female archangels?"

"I'm afraid not," said Sophia.

"In that case," said the young woman in a firm voice, "I must insist that God is a male chauvinist pig."

She was applauded by some, but others felt that they had received a blow, and that she had gone too far.

Sophia turned pale; she clenched her fists, drew back a step, and adopted the fighting stance of Jem Mace.

"Come, dearie," said Adelaide, and took her out of there.

Chapter
6

THEY CAME from all over the city, from the Bronx, from Queens, from the suburbs, from Connecticut, New Jersey, from as far away as Pennsylvania, to hear the Rusty Mops, the greatest rock group in the world. Already the vast amphitheater was filled to capacity, and the streets leading to the Garden were black with people still waiting to get in. They milled about, humming like a horde of angry insects.

Inside the Garden itself, the heavy air seemed charged with tension, as though an oncoming storm were about to break. A nervous excitement rose from the crowd, flickering upward from the floor like static electricity. At the same time, unlike the stillness which precedes a storm, the noise was baffling, attacking the senses from every direction, as twenty thousand young people—plump, teen-aged girls, long-haired boys, wide-eyed teeny-boppers, black dudes in furs, middle-aged ladies with disheveled hair, all shouted, swayed, stamped, pushed about, and exchanged excited glances.

Michael George gazed about him in bewilderment. Smoke rose toward the high-domed ceiling from thousands of cigarettes, the heavy, sweet smell of pot hung in the air. Psychedelic lights swam about through the smoky, night-dim interior, blue, red, yellow, and white, lighting up a face, a swirl of color, bare arms, bare shoulders, naked flesh . . . like something (he thought) out of Hieronymus Bosch, or Gustave Doré.

Could this be what Hell is like? thought Sophia, clinging close to Adelaide.

The members of the warm-up band were already on the stage, but no one seemed to notice them; the steady sound of their drumming merely melted into the general hubbub. The band retired presently, taking their instruments with them; and after a slight wait, during which the vast amphitheater grew gradually still and the tension mounted even higher, the Rusty Mops themselves appeared; and the crowd screamed. High and shrill, the scream was followed by a hoarse howling, like a storm of wind suddenly let loose, a tornado of sound, violent, mindless, and meaningless.

All the lights were turned onto the stage, where Jingle himself, painted and smeared, half-naked, half bespangled, part satyr, part nymph, went through his lascivious prancing and flaunting, up and down the stage, snarling and shrieking into a microphone held against his lips, while the rest of the group, behind him, kept up a steady, monotonous beat, a riff repeated over and over. The words of the song, as well as the melody, were indistinguishable, and even unheard over the howling and crying of the audience. "Good heavens," cried Michael George to Aaron Aaron, "this is simply bedlam!"

The composer shrugged, an inscrutable smile on his lips. "I never promised you Brahms," he said.

Sophia stared in horror at the stage, at the sprawling, jerking, androgynous figure of the great Jingle. What was he trying to convey? Was he a man seducing a woman? or a woman seducing a man? He was both, she thought, at the same time—the ultimate in depravity. Next to her a large, bare-bosomed girl let out a deep, chewing-gum-scented sigh. "Oh, God," she breathed. "He's the most!"

Elsewhere in the auditorium the critic for the *Saturday Review-World* nudged her companion, the reviewer for *Time* Magazine. "Delightfully vicious, isn't he?" she remarked happily, to which her companion, three years out of Harvard, replied, "Great art! Great art!"

"It is, isn't it!" she agreed. "So deliciously bestial. So raunchy!"

"Indeed, indeed," murmured the young man from *Time*.

Unlike Sophia, Buckthorne felt quite at ease, and very much interested. In fact, he believed that the entire experience was opening his mind to new horizons, and that he had come upon a whole new aspect of what had been puzzling him. It is not the music, he said to himself; for the music, as such, is trifling. It is not the lyrics, which in any case cannot be heard; when they are, they turn out to

ROBERT NATHAN

be either bathetic or vulgar. Nor is it the beat, although
I admit that it has a certain hypnotic quality; it rules the
pulse, and thereby the flow of blood to the brain. Nor is
it the antics of that silly clown who cavorts on the stage
like some ancient Greek's idea of a demon, luring the
nubile girls and hungry boys to sexual fantasies. . . .

No, by Hecate, he thought, it is the crowd which has
hypnotized itself! It is the audience, whose tensions, finally
exploding, relieve themselves in a mass orgasm.

Of course! A mass orgasm. Was there an answer for
him there? In the mass, rather than in the individual?
In the porridge into which man was cooking himself?
Uncertain, but thoughtful, he started to push his way
toward the nearest exit. But he was too late; the vast
crowd outside had managed by sheer crush of numbers to
force the doors, and were pouring into the already over-
crowded amphitheater. And in no time at all, a new note
was added to the overwhelming noise: cries of anger,
shouts and screams resounded here and there; people,
risen in fright from their seats, surged this way and that,
fists and sticks rose and fell, the flash of a knife was seen.
A thin line of police moved in, and was swallowed up in
the tumult. Several women and children were trampled;
and Jingle, after one stupefied look at the scene before
him, turned and rushed from the stage, followed by his
terrified companions.

Sophia, torn from her friend's side, cowered between
two overturned rows of benches while the riot raged
around and above her. She was bewildered; nothing in her

experience had prepared her for anything like it, and she could only close her eyes, press her hands over her ears, and pray. Where was Hugo?

All at once, a voice sharp as a whiplash cut through the tumult above her, and a strong arm lifted her to her feet. "Come," someone said, and opening her eyes, she found herself once again face to face with the young stranger from the park. Not only was she surprised to see him, she was even more surprised by his apparent elation; he seemed to be enjoying himself. "This way," he said, "and hurry."

By what means he guided her through the mass of struggling bodies, she didn't know; it was not until she found herself outside in the cool night air that she regained her senses enough to stop, rearrange her dress, set her bonnet back on her head, and to extend her hand. "You again," she said. "How strange. How do you do?"

Police cars, their sirens wailing, were converging on the Garden, and Buckthorne drew her down a side street out of the way. "That was a close thing," he said. "Are you all right?"

"Oh, yes," she said, "quite. And thank you very much. Though I don't know what I'd have done . . ."

He regarded her gravely, but with a certain appreciation. "I rather think we could both do with a drink," he said. "Don't you?"

"Yes, I do," she said. "That would be lovely."

They sat in the Oak Room of the Plaza, sipping whiskey and soda and munching on chicken sandwiches.

ROBERT NATHAN

Sophia had allowed Buckthorne to order for her; and
although she had rather expected a raspberry syrup or at
most a negus, she found the whiskey not unpleasant. "I
have never tasted this before," she admitted. "What is it?"

"It is a drink made from malt," said Buckthorne. "A
natural grain."

She nodded, satisfied. "It must be very wholesome,"
she said.

Buckthorne sat back and studied her. What was there
about her that both attracted and disturbed him? Was she,
indeed, an innocent?—an Edwardian, a Victorian out of
place?

"What happened to your dog?" he asked. "Did you
find him again?"

Sophia bit her lip. To tell the truth, for the moment
at least she had quite forgotten Hugo. But what *had* happened to him? He'd been late before, of course—like at
that set-to with Adelaide. But where had he been when
she needed him the most?

"Yes," she said calmly, "I found him." And she added,
lightly,

"Bad dog."

As a matter of fact, at the time of the riot in the Garden,
Hugo had been trying to sniff out the hiding place of a
bomb left somewhere in the TWA terminal at Kennedy
Airport. He had failed to find it; twenty minutes after he
had trotted out of the building with his tail in the air, it
blew up, killing and injuring thirty-seven waiting passengers and attendants. But Sophia had no way of knowing that.

Buckthorne gazed at her thoughtfully, through narrowed lids. There was something peculiar about that dog, he thought: as well as about its mistress. "Look here," he said finally, "you don't belong here, do you?"

"N—no," she said, hesitatingly. "I'm . . . from out of town."

"I thought so," said Buckthorne. "Actually, so am I." And leaning across the table, he held out his hand. They smiled at each other.

"Have you ever been here before?" he asked.

"No," she said. "Funnily enough . . . no."

He nodded, satisfied. "Well, I have," he declared. "In the twenties. Prohibition . . . It was a fun city then."

Sophia gave him a startled glance. In the twenties? That was fifty years ago. And he was only twenty-odd himself, from the looks of it.

"Yes," he said thoughtfully, "there was a lot to do in those days." His eyes took on a dreamy, faraway look. "Do you know what we did?" he asked. "We used to hire a victoria—a 'seagoing hack' we used to call it—and drive around the park all night. And watch the dawn come up, and never go to bed at all."

"Oh, how lovely," sighed Sophia. He had read about it, she supposed, in a book by—whom? Fitzgerald? She had no idea; her reading had stopped with Chesterton. "I should like that," she said.

Chapter
7

"WHAT FUN!" exclaimed Sophia, sinking back in the open carriage as it pulled away from the hack stand opposite the hotel. It smelled of warm rubber and old wood, of worn upholstery, of stables and oiled leather. But once in the park, in the damp night air, the smell of grass and leaves took over.

A few cars passed them from behind, their red taillights vanishing in the distance or around the next curve; but for the most part they rolled quietly along except for the clop-clop of the horse's hooves on the asphalt. Between lampposts, the roadway was dark; shadows rose up on either side, hung over them like trees. Buckthorne settled the carriage robe around Sophia's knees; it smelled faintly of camphor. "Thank you," she said.

"You are always thanking me," said Buckthorne, "and for nothing, really."

"Was it nothing to get me out of that dreadful place?"

asked Sophia. "With people screaming all around me?"

Michael George turned around and looked back at them. "Ah," he said. "Were you at the Garden, by any chance?"

"Yes," said Buckthorne shortly. "We were."

"So was I," said Michael. "And I had a hard time getting out."

He paused for a moment, before turning back. "I suppose," he ventured, "that you young people care for that sort of thing?"

"Heavens no," said Sophia. "Not at all."

Michael nodded. "And what about that creature on the stage?" he inquired.

"A lost soul," stated Buckthorne with satisfaction.

" 'All hope abandon, ye who enter here,' " quoted Michael, and returned to his driving.

Buckthorne's eyebrows rose. "We have a poet with us," he remarked.

"Dante," said Sophia. "*The Divine Comedy:* Canto 3, of 'The Inferno.' '*Lasciate ogni speranza voi ch'entrate. . . . Per me si va ne la città dolente, per me si va ne l'etterno dolore . . .*' "

Buckthorne gazed at her in astonishment. "I say," he declared, "that was rather good."

"I was quite a long time in Italy," said Sophia. "In Rome mostly; and later in Assisi."

"It is colder in the park than I thought," said Buckthorne uneasily. "Would you mind if I shared some of your carriage robe?"

"Not in the least," said Sophia; "here—let me . . ."

And she tucked half the carriage robe around him. "Thank you," said Buckthorne, and settled back against her. But after a moment or two, he moved away again. Her shoulder was soft, and cool, and should have been comfortable, but for some reason was not.

"You're a strange girl," he said after a while. "For a time, I placed you somewhere in the Middle West. But now, I take you to be English: a rector's daughter, perhaps?"

She laughed gaily; her laughter was light, like a running brook. "No," she said, "not a rector's daughter. But I have spent some time in England, visiting the cathedrals."

"Have you?" he said. "And did you visit Canterbury, where Becket was murdered?"

"Of course," she said, but he thought she sounded a bit subdued. "He was martyred," she declared.

"And the Tower?"

"Certainly not," she said. "Did you?"

"Often," he said.

"How odd," she murmured. "That dreadful pile."

From the coachman's box, Michael George inquired, "Shall we follow the usual route, making the circle, across and down the West Side? If so, I must tell you that there are one or two places where it would be wise to proceed at a smarter pace, possibly even a gallop."

"Not to worry," said Buckthorne. "Besides, we are in no hurry. I have something else in mind."

And he ordered the coachman to leave the park and strike west to the Hudson. "We should be off the island before sunup," he declared. "Do you think your animal can make it?"

Michael George looked startled. "It's a long drive," he said uncertainly. "He might, and then again he mightn't."

"I'm sure he will," said Buckthorne heartily; and turning to Sophia, "Would you like to have breakfast in Van Cortlandt Park?" he asked. "Sitting on the grass, in the early sunlight? Al fresco?"

"That would be lovely," said Sophia.

"Drive on," said Buckthorne.

Michael made a gesture of resignation. It would be a strange adventure, he thought; and certainly, what with one thing and another, a fitting way to end what had been a strange day altogether. Besides, it should pay very well. He shrugged his shoulders. " 'Theirs not to reason why,' " he intoned, and set his course westward.

Sophia smiled. "Now it's Kipling," she announced; and snuggled down into her half of the blanket.

Just before they left the park, they heard a muffled scream somewhere in the dark behind them. Sophia gave a shiver, and clutched at Buckthorne's hand. "Oh dear," she exclaimed. "Oughtn't we to go back? Some poor woman . . ."

Buckthorne shook his head. "It is already too late," he said. "And besides, it is only a drop in the bucket."

But he continued to hold her hand, which, like the rest of her, was soft yet firm, and gave him prickles up his arm. "Whoever she was," he said, "she has already been raped, and had her throat cut. Some wretched fellow has had his jollies with her."

Michael George half turned in his seat. His jollies? He was surprised; that was a phrase he hadn't heard for fifty years at least.

Buckthorne went on bitterly:

"It is the same all over the city," he said, "and all over the world. Wherever you look, death."

"I know," said Sophia sadly. "But Mr. Buckthorne . . ."

"Buck," said Buckthorne.

"Well," said Sophia uncertainly, "if you like . . . But what I mean is Why? Why, Buck? Why just now, at this time in the world?"

"There has always been violence," said Buckthorne slowly, "war, death, and destruction. Ever since Cain slew Abel. But always in the past . . ."

She interrupted him. "If Adam and Eve had never been tempted by the Serpent," she said stoutly, "there would be no murders."

"Yes, yes," he replied impatiently, "and there'd have been no Cain and Abel either. Only the witches, east of Eden."

"Witches?" asked Sophia, puzzled. "I know of no witches. Adam and Eve were the only . . ."

Buckthorne smiled wearily. "And whom do you think Cain married?" he demanded. "A sister?" He waved away the suggestion. "It is of no consequence," he said. "I was about to say that always in the past there was some sense of order to the violence: great wars, pestilence, famine, political unrest, private feuds; but always there were islands of tranquillity somewhere else, where one could do one's work. While Napoleon ravaged Europe, the English were enjoying themselves in their customary way. So were the Sioux, in America.

"But now, no one is safe anywhere; some lunacy is loose, senseless and murderous. What is one more young woman raped and butchered after dark—or even before lunch? The thing is—we must stop the slaughter."

"Yes, oh, yes," cried Sophia, sitting up, her eyes shining with excitement. Presently, however, her face fell. "But how?" she asked. "What is at the root of all this madness?"

Buckthorne sighed. "We don't know," he admitted. "It is, frankly, beyond us. Perhaps some influence from another galaxy, another system . . ."

Sophia shook her head. "I know very little about other systems," she said. "Surely we can find something closer to home? Satan . . ."

"Forget Satan," said Buckthorne simply. "He is as upset as you are."

Sophia looked at him in surprise. "He is?" she asked curiously. "Do you really think so?"

"I do," said Buckthorne firmly. "I know it for a fact."

And seeing Sophia's eyebrows rise in suspicion, he went on hurriedly,

"After all, it stands to reason. It's one thing to seduce the innocent and corrupt the good. But in a world where

ROBERT NATHAN

everyone was evil, what would there be left for him to
do?"

Sophia nodded slowly, and sank back in her seat. "I
hadn't thought of that," she conceded. "Just as in a world
where there were no more souls left to save . . ."

Her voice dwindled off. "Well, then," she said, "if not
Satan . . ."

Buckthorne shrugged impatiently. "A microbe, perhaps," he said. "Of an unknown strain. An undetectable
virus. Some malfunction of the spleen . . ."

"I know nothing about microbes," said Sophia, "or the
spleen either. Are you a doctor?"

He hesitated for a moment. "In a sense," he said,
"though not a medical doctor. That is to say, I am interested in science. For instance, I have learned, just recently,
that the mass orgasm . . ."

"Although grounded in the classics," said Sophia, "I
did not receive a scientific education. What is an orgasm?"

He gaped at her incredulously. *I don't believe it,* he said
to himself. *What have we here?*

"I'm sorry," said Sophia, noting his consternation. "I've
only been a woman for such a short time."

"In that case," said Buckthorne, rallying, "I might
someday perhaps be able to teach you . . ."

Sophia felt a delicious apprehension, her skin crawled,
she trembled, and was seized with a slight vertigo. "Lead
us not into temptation," she whispered under her breath,
"and deliver us from evil . . ."

Buckthorne experienced a sudden sharp pain in his

arm which he had allowed to rest negligently across Sophia's shoulders. "Drat these old carriages," he muttered; "they are full of rheumatism."

Sophia said nothing. She was troubled, in a way she didn't understand. She didn't even know why.

Chapter

8

HERE AND THERE along the river which shone like dull pewter in the dark, the neon lights of Jersey flashed on and flickered off. The night hung above them with its stars, cloudless, immense; while beside the couple in the cab, over their heads, rose the tall apartment buildings —dark, brooding ramparts of the city. In how many such buildings, and in the narrow streets between, were scenes of violence taking place at the very moment they passed by? What anguished cries, shouts, oaths, screams were silenced by those walls, diminished, muffled by the dark, unheard by the unhearing?

Buckthorne and Sophia sat in silence, busy with their thoughts. In Buckthorne's case, these had to do with his project; and he wondered uneasily what he was doing in a victoria, late at night, beside the Hudson River, on his way to the Bronx. He had discovered something, but what to do with it, how to use it . . .? Would he find the answer in Van Cortlandt Park? or even by the Sawmill River? He thought it unlikely. There had been other meetings he should have attended before he left the city: a luncheon at the National Institute of Arts and Letters, for instance, where he could have met and argued with the foremost artists and critics of the Establishment; or a lecture at the Forum, where he would have mingled with bankers and generals, foreign secretaries, premiers, presidents—even nuclear scientists. Not that they would have told him anything, of course.

Was he making a fool of himself? If he was, it couldn't be helped. There was something about Sophia which tempted him beyond anything; tempted him, yet filled him with gentleness too, and with a kind of awe. He had never experienced anything remotely like it; he wanted to impress her, to shine for her, to make her laugh and sigh and weep, to possess her and to protect her at the same time, to ravish her and worship her. It was extremely confusing.

Sophia's mind was equally confused. She tried to think about her duty, her mission, but her thoughts kept straying to the stranger at her side. After all, she had been a woman for such a short time; what should she know about a woman's feelings?—or, for that matter, a man's? A man's ways in the world. She stole a glance at Buckthorne, silent and morose beside her. He was a man, she supposed; wasn't he? So then?

But the fact was she was experiencing feelings entirely new, and altogether unexpected. They were woman-feelings, she guessed, and she tried to understand them. Why should Buckthorne appear beautiful to her? Certainly he lacked that classic, that almost austere symmetry to which she was accustomed; his features, though handsome if taken one by one, were in fact out of patience with each other—the mouth too thin for the chin, the nose too large for the eyes, the brow too narrow; yet the whole had a charm, even a kind of beauty—a little cruel, perhaps . . . or was it merely cold?—that caught at her somewhere in the vicinity of the throat. Why should that be? Was there something in a woman—in womanhood—that was attracted to the unsymmetrical in man? How silly! But there it was. Buckthorne was dark, proud, taciturn, and—yes—cruel-looking. Arrogant too, she thought; and even (the word flashed through her mind) saturnine. She remembered the serene faces of her friends—faces which could take on an expression of severity when called for, but were more often joyful and triumphant. Buckthorne, she thought, had probably never been joyful in his life; triumphant, perhaps—but over what? Some woman like herself? she wondered; and felt a moment of utter desolation, mixed with a sudden strange excitement which caused her to blush and bite her lip.

And for the first time, she felt a sympathy for all women, and believed that she understood the young female who had decided to run for Congress from Madame Berthe's House of Beauty. How vulnerable we are, she thought, if instead of beauty and order we are attracted to what is ugly and malicious. Have we no power of choice? Is there something altogether male, arrogant, and rapacious, to which we must offer ourselves like virgins to Moloch or Yumchac? Such things had always seemed to her —for so she had been taught—to be the work of the Devil; but she was no longer sure. Perhaps it was, rather, a human flaw; in which case, perhaps God was, after all, a . . .

She shuddered violently, and began to recite a Rosary through clenched teeth, even though the Rosary was part of a later schooling, and unknown to her in her youth. But then in her youth she had been as innocent as a cloud in the sky, and there had been no Buckthorne.

In any event, new or old, it helped to comfort her, and she grew quieter in her feelings. Woman, in essence, was still inviolable, except to the Holy Ghost; and it was the essence, rather than the vulnerable fringe, that she was meant to explore. As well as man, of course—who, being God's creation, must also be good at the core. Perhaps, as Buckthorne said, it was a virus.

And she reached over and timidly touched his hand.

It was just as they were passing under the George Washington Bridge that a gang of nearly a dozen hoodlums appeared before them, lined up across the driveway. There was no mistaking their intention, which was to do as much harm as possible both to the carriage and its occupants. Michael George sighed gently, and brought his equipage to a stop; he sat, white, miserable, and resigned, uncertainly twirling his whip, while Sophia, shocked out of her reverie, stared in consternation at what confronted

them. She had perhaps a moment in which to wish for
Hugo, before Buckthorne, brought so rudely back to
reality by the sudden arrest of their journey, rose from his
seat and with an oath, and slowly stepping down from the
carriage, declared,

"Leave this to me."

So saying, he advanced with a measured pace inexor-
ably upon the hoodlums, who first awaited him with
sneers, brandishing knives and clubs; but presently turned
nervous, began to twitch, and finally—after one close look
at Buckthorne's face—turned and fled in terror and utter
ruin from the spot.

Sophia, watching in amazement, but seeing only the
back of Buckthorne's head, could not imagine what had
frightened them to such an extent; or believe that the face
they had glimpsed was something they would never forget,
but would wake up screaming in the night, remembering.

And in fact, when Buckthorne returned to the carriage,
his face was still shining with such a fierce light that for
a moment she trembled. Was it a holy light? Or the contrary? And yet—what a divine rage!

Yes, she thought: that was it, that was what was needed.
From whatever quarter. A divine rage.

As the carriage continued on its way and the horse
plodded patiently on, Michael George stared straight
ahead, his lips pursed in a soundless whistle. He was
shaken, but also curiously elated. He too had seen Buckthorne's face, and there had been nothing divine about it.

"For by excess of evil, evil dies." Santayana had been

right after all then, without knowing it. Or had he known it?

But Sophia, satisfied, comforted, slept for the rest of the journey, her head cradled against Buckthorne's shoulder.

Chapter
9

THE CARRIAGE rested in a field off the road in Van Cortlandt Park; released from the traces, the horse grazed peacefully, while Michael George, in the back seat, worked on his journal. The sun shone; a short way off, on the carriage robe spread out for them on the grass, Buckthorne and Sophia were enjoying a breakfast of honey cakes, hard-boiled eggs, and hot chocolate put up for them by the Plaza.

Michael wrote in his journal:

The more we discover, the less we know. According to Dr. Ponnamperuna of Ceylon, the universe—which was at that time a huge cloud or ball of hydrogen gas—exploded some thirteen billion years ago; and some 8.3 billion years later, the planet earth congealed from the dust of that explosion.

That is the sort of answer which leaves only questions behind it. From what did this hydrogen cloud develop?

and where did it hang? Was it there at the beginning—or was there an earlier beginning still?

So there they are, the nonsensical questions. How can we think of a beginning—or an end—to eternity? Or to time, which sits in eternity like a frozen sea, yesterday, today, and tomorow all spread out together . . . the fourth dimension, that dimension beyond our senses, comprehensible to us mathematically, but in which, unlike in our more familiar third dimension, we have no power of movement: we simply are?

And where, in such a primeval explosion and in the slow unfolding and transformation which led to the production of nucleic and amino acids, and thereby to the stuff of life itself, was there room for good and evil?

Yesterday I watched a depraved young man perform upon a stage. He was a transvestite, or a hermaphrodite, or one of the "new breed" open to all comers. And I was reminded that the fall of cities and of empires was always preceded and accompanied by such performances, from Babylon to Berlin. Shall we, too, find written upon our walls the ominous words: *Mene, Mene, Tekel, Upharsin?*

For there is, without doubt, such a thing as evil. I have even seen its face; strangely enough, at the time, it wore the expression of a hero. And what I take to be good, may in the end turn out to be its victim. Yet, where would that leave God, Who is thought to be the Personification of good itself?

Except that I cannot conceive of God as being a creature, a form, or even an idea, or anything that the mind of man can grasp. And yet . . . and yet . . . What if all our science is illusion? What if there are actually angels and devils here on earth? Eating honey cakes and drinking chocolate in a meadow, on the grass?

"Do you know," said Buckthorne, "I am enjoying myself enormously. And I was not expected to at all."

"I too," said Sophia, biting into a hard-boiled egg, "am having a lovely time. Funnily enough, I'm sure I wasn't meant to have. But it *is* such a splendid morning, and to be out of the city—"

" 'Alexandria, thou mighty city,' " intoned Buckthorne, waving his cup of chocolate in the direction of Manhattan.

"Is that Luke?" asked Sophia. "Or Matthew?"

"It is neither," replied Buckthorne; "it is Anatole France, and it is from his novel, *Thaïs.* In it, the monk Paphnutius denounces Alexandria, the home of *Thaïs,* the courtesan."

He appeared embarrassed for a moment. "Actually," he said, "those exact words do not appear in the book, but in the opera *Thaïs* which Massenet composed, based upon the novel. I admit it is less than a literal translation of Massenet's phrase, but it expresses my feelings at the moment."

And he sang in a light clear baritone,

"Alexandrie, Alexandrie, où je suis né, dans le péché."

"I believe," said Sophia, wrinkling her brow, "that Thaïs became a nun, and died in the odor of sanctity. In fact, there is a question whether one of our lesser saints . . ."

"And the monk cursed God," said Buckthorne, "and became a demon. Poor Paphnutius—or, as he is called in the opera, Athanael—that being a name easier to set to music, and less trouble for the singer. Not a real demon, of course: rather a sort of minor djinn.

"No one," he added proudly, "can simply become a demon. Unlike the situation of your saints, one has to be born to it."

Suddenly his expression changed to one of bewilderment. "Do you realize," he said slowly, "that we have been speaking of 'ours' and 'yours'? Almost as though . . ."

"Please," said Sophia hurriedly. "I know. Don't let's go on about it."

He nodded thoughtfully. "Under the circumstances," he agreed, "that might be best. Because, if . . ."

She put her finger to his lips. "Hush," she said urgently. "Don't." And, before she could withdraw her finger, he had kissed it. Beyond a sudden sting as from a burn, she suffered no ill effects. "Forgive me," he said. "It was an impulse."

Sophia blushed and turned away. "I think I will have another honey cake," she declared.

The Seraph Azrael went to look for Gabriel. He found the great archangel seated on a cloud, gazing gloomily at earth spread out below him like a checkerboard. "Our girl," said Azrael, "has had a bit of an accident, I'm afraid. It seems that she's met up with someone."

"Indeed?" said Gabriel indifferently. "Well—wasn't

she supposed to, you know, meet up with people? Or something?"

"Tall, dark, and—if you ask me—right out of Hell?" asked the seraph.

Gabriel straightened up with a startled look on his face. "That, of course," he said, "is a different kettle of fish altogether. We shall have to see about *that!* Can't have that sort of thing, you know," he added. "Dreadful complications, and all."

"Exactly," agreed Azrael. "Shall we call her back?"

The archangel hesitated. "If we do," he said thoughtfully, "she might not come, of course. I mean to say—if she really *is* . . . No, I'm afraid we shall have to go after her.

"How many guards are left?"

"Only Hugo, I'm afraid," said the seraph. "All the other chaps are completely engaged."

Gabriel nodded. "Send for Hugo then," he said. "That is, if you can find him."

"Righto," said Azrael.

"Meanwhile," said Gabriel unhappily, "we could always thunder a bit."

Since neither of them wanted to return to the city, Buckthorne and Sophia decided to continue their journey into the country; Buckthorne because for the first time in his memory he felt happy, and Sophia because she enjoyed the sunlight and the fresh air, the sweet smells, and being with Buckthorne. As for Michael George, he considered it a privilege under the circumstances, and was eager to see how it would all turn out.

At noon, with the horse tied up to a birch tree, and Michael asleep in the shade of an elm, Sophia and Buckthorne sat on the grassy bank of the Bronx River, and dabbled their feet in the shallow, brown water. "You know," said Buckthorne reflectively, "you are a very pretty girl, Sophia."

"I am not a girl," she said, and sighed.

"I know," he admitted gravely. "But even so."

"And you," she said, "are frightfully brave."

He gazed at her in surprise. "Brave?" he said. "What makes you think so?"

"Because of the way you faced those dreadful men last night."

"Oh, that," he said negligently. "That was nothing."

"But they turned and ran like anything!"

He smiled reminiscently. "I know," he said. "I terrified them." And he added simply, "I have all kinds of faces, you see."

Sophia sighed again. "I have only one face," she said. "And I'm afraid it's rather plain."

"It's beautiful," said Buckthorne.

"I believe it's considered cinquocento," said Sophia hopefully, "or possibly Burne-Jones."

He studied her gravely, turning her face from side to side. "Yes," he said at last, "I can see that. The eighties, the nineties . . . what a delightful era! What good times we had! So much to do; I can tell you, we were kept busy.

... So much stupidity, so much hypocrisy. But all open and aboveboard, nothing incomprehensible, like the present violence."

"For us, too," said Sophia, "it was a pleasant time. The home front was secure; there was only the heathen . . ."

Buckthorne suddenly laughed aloud. "Do you know," he said, "I believe that we are probably here on the same errand!"

Sophia nodded her head. "I've thought so too," she admitted shyly.

"Then why not join forces?" he asked boldly.

But she was wiser than he. "I don't think They'd like it," she said.

It was Buckthorne's turn to sigh. "Yes," he agreed, "I can see what you mean. Belial . . ."

"Gabriel . . ."

"No," he said reluctantly, "they'd never understand." He was silent for a moment, lost in gloomy thoughts. "To tell you the truth," he said at last, "I don't understand it myself."

"I suppose," said Sophia uncertainly, "that the end justifies the means?"

Buckthorne stared at her in surprise. "What?" he exclaimed. "Do they believe that in H . . . where you come from?"

"Why yes," she said. And then, in equal surprise, "Don't you?"

He laughed gaily. "Of course," he announced. "It is the very cornerstone of our belief. The standard, as it were, of the entire apparatus." However, he soon turned serious again, and gazed moodily at the little stream in which they were kicking their feet. "It would mean a real meeting of minds at the summit," he said, "and that hasn't taken place since the Creation. It would mean at very least a détente, with an exchange of ambassadors, and so forth . . . and that would never do. Can you imagine Beelzebub being welcomed in Heaven?"

"Or Raphael in Hell?" giggled Sophia.

Suddenly they both burst out laughing, clutching each other like naughty children. A moment later, their lips met and clung, despite a burning sensation on the one hand, and frostbite on the other.

"Angel!" breathed Buckthorne, in despair.

"Betrayer!" murmured Sophia fondly.

A distant peal of thunder awoke Michael George, who gazed about him in alarm. But he must have dreamed it, he thought, for the sky was blue and clear, the sun was shining overhead, and the shadow of leaves fell gently on him as before.

Chapter

10

HOWEVER, Sophia had heard, and drawing away from her companion's embrace, she stared up at him in fright. "Buck," she whispered, "They've seen us. They know."

She gave a little gasp. "Now," she said, "if Hugo comes, it won't be as a friend."

"Mmm," muttered Buckthorne. "That could create a difficulty." And he thought uncomfortably of Saint George and the dragon. "I could turn myself into a toad or something unnoticeable," he said, "but the truth is, I don't want to lose you. Damn it, Sophia—I've only just found you!

"And something else," he added, suddenly embarrassed. "Something I'd never found before."

"What?" she asked, looking up at him, as shy as he, but imploring.

"Love," he said simply.

"Me too," she whispered.

"Well, then," he said bravely; but a moment later, in exasperation,

"I don't even know what it is, really. I don't at all. It's a . . . a miracle!"

Once again she placed a quick finger on his lips. "Not that word," she said. "It will only anger Them."

Buckthorne took a deep breath, and let it out again. "All right," he said quietly. "What are we to do?"

"We must seek some sort of sanctuary," she said. "Perhaps a convent."

"A convent?" cried Buckthorne. "Are you mad? Sophia —what would I do in a convent?"

"Oh," she said, "not for you, my dear. You have no reason to be afraid; your people have no cause to be angry. *You* haven't done anything unusual; whilst I . . ."

"But I have!" he exclaimed. "I've been *happy*. And I haven't stopped the violence, or found anything . . . at least, not anything very much . . . Except you," he added miserably.

"You're very sweet," she said. "Thank you for that."

She gazed around her for a moment, with a bewildered expression. "Oh, dear," she murmured helplessly. But a moment later, gathering herself together, she turned back to him, smiling bravely. "Chin up!" she exclaimed. "This will all be over someday. And after I'm forgiven . . ."

"And how many thousand years will that take?" he asked forlornly.

She smiled at him as brightly as she could. "What difference does it make?" she asked. "We have all eternity."

"Damn eternity!" cried Buckthorne violently. "I want it now!"

Nevertheless, there appeared to be no help for it; he

could offer no alternative, and half an hour later the victoria drew up before the gates of the Convent of the Sisters of Piety in Bronxville. "Good-bye, dear friend," Sophia whispered, and with a tremulous smile, stepped down from the carriage, and knocked at the convent gates, while Buckthorne waited anxiously around the corner out of sight.

The young novice who came to the door gazed at Sophia round-eyed before going off to summon the mother superior. Middle-aged, serene, the nun's patient gaze studied Sophia from head to toe, before she reluctantly shook her head.

"My dear," she said, "I am sorry; but we cannot take you in."

"Not take me in?" cried Sophia in bewilderment. "But that's unheard of! You must; it is your duty."

And in tones of outrage, she exclaimed,

"I demand Sanctuary."

The mother superior nodded her head sympathetically. "I know," she said quietly. "And if it were myself alone ... But there are orders. We have been told ..."

She glanced at Sophia, and then away. "You see," she said, almost apologetically, "it seems that there is a fallen angel somewhere in the neighborhood, and we cannot be too careful."

So saying, she crossed herself, and while the young novice looked on in wonder and terror, slowly closed the door in Sophia's face.

Sophia returned to the carriage; she was pale, and her

voice trembled. "There is only one thing left for us," she announced. "We must hide."

"Hide?" cried Buckthorne incredulously. "From God and the Devil both? Earth isn't wide enough, nor the oceans, either."

Sophia's eyes filled with tears. And gazing upward, she murmured piteously,

"Is there no shelter for us anywhere?"

"If I might make a suggestion," said Michael George from his seat on the coachman's box, "I have a small cottage less than ten miles from here, which I inherited from my mother, and in which, from time to time, I take a small holiday. It is modest, to say the least; but it would serve to shelter you, though not, I am afraid, for very long, if, as I understand it, the powers that be are after you."

"Where is this cottage?" asked Buckthorne impatiently.

"It is hidden away in Hartsdale," said Michael, "in a small wood behind the cemetery."

Buckthorne turned to Sophia. "How long do we have?" he asked. "Before . . . you know . . .?"

"Perhaps an hour," she said uncertainly. "Perhaps less."

"Very well," declared Buckthorne firmly. And to Michael,

"Drive on! And hurry."

"I have only one horse," said Michael, "but I will do the best I can."

Chapter
11

SEATED before the empty fireplace in Michael George's little cottage in Hartsdale, Buckthorne and Sophia devoured the last of the hard-boiled eggs, and drank some milk from the refrigerator. They said very little, but gazed at each other with grief and longing. "When I think," murmured Buckthorne, "that it was I who got you into this . . .!"

Sophia smiled mistily, and shook her head. "You were only being gallant," she said. "And anyway, I wouldn't have wanted it otherwise, no matter what."

"I suppose that ought to make me feel better," said Buckthorne, "but somehow it doesn't."

"But just imagine," exclaimed Sophia, "if we'd never met!" And holding hands, they smiled gravely at each other, across the few feet of empty air which separated them.

In a corner near the window, in the slanting light of

late afternoon, Michael George was writing in his journal. What curious tricks memory plays on us, he wrote. I cannot remember the days spent in Paris with Stephen and Rosemary Benét, or what Thomas Wolfe and I talked about the day he came to visit me; and yet I remember so vividly waiting, a child of five, for the arrival of my friend Alfred Jaretzki at a hotel in Vermont; and how I jumped about for joy, crying "ray, Jay!" He must have been seven at the time, or perhaps eight; and for years he was a hero in my mind. And my cousin Stanley Halle ... what a hero *he* was! so tall and well-dressed, at fourteen. He died long ago. But Jay is still alive, and an ornament to the legal profession—retired by now, I should think. I haven't seen him for forty years.

The clouds are closing down around me; my world is drifting farther and farther back into the mists of the past. It was a world strangely unlike this present world —a world of faith rather than cynicism, of hope rather than despair. Granted that the faith was misplaced, and the hope without reason, yet we were happier in our ignorance. For we believed in God, and the future of mankind, which nobody believes in anymore.

I am probably very near death, and I wonder: how do I feel about it? The answer, I fear, must be somewhat equivocal; I am not afraid of being dead, but I am afraid of dying. That final moment must indeed be agonizing, both to the mind, and to the body—unless, of course, it occurs during a period of unconsciousness. But even then ... does the brain, perhaps, know? And does one—as

Shakespeare asked—dream for a while, with no chance of ever waking, and perhaps badly?

Only the spirit can ride it out without a qualm. That supposes, of course, that there is indeed a spirit beyond the flesh, beyond the nerves, bones, muscles, organs, beyond the cells of the brain: some sense of self, of being, not dependent upon oxygen. Is there? I think so . . . I do not know.

I was in love once, long ago, with a great beauty; and what's more, a truly loving woman. Such women were hard to find, even in those days, when love was something to be treasured. She died—fortunately, as it turned out, although it did not seem so at the time; for she was older than I was, and by now would have lost her beauty and even her teeth. But I often wonder if I shall ever find her again in the hereafter. During the height of our affair, it seemed as though I must: as though love such as ours couldn't die, that it couldn't, after all, count for nothing in the overall scheme of things. Yet, on the other hand, when I think of the infinite multitudes of the dead; how their spirits must lie in eternity like innumerable grains of sand on a beach, and to seek and find one single one in that endless expanse . . .

I too am old now, but I do not feel old in spirit—in that part of me which could, conceivably, love as deeply as before, though not with the same anguish. So perhaps, there may be, after all, something to look forward to . . .

After brooding over this for a moment or two, he closed his journal, and turning to Sophia, asked her if she thought that he might meet his long-dead love in Heaven. Sophia, rousing herself from her contemplation of her companion, seemed uncertain. "Was she a Catholic?" she asked. "Or a Church of England?"

Michael replied that she had been a Jewess. "Oh," said Sophia, "in that case, I'm afraid I wouldn't know."

"Yet you yourself," said Michael gently, "are Hebrew in nature."

"I am?" exclaimed Sophia in surprise.

"The first mention of angels," said Michael, "is found neither in the Egyptian, Sumerian, Babylonian, Greek, or Roman documents, but in the Old Testament. As a matter of fact, for a long while you were nameless: such signatures as Michael, Gabriel, Raphael, are comparatively recent. The cherubim who stood before the Garden with flaming swords, the angel who wrestled with Jacob, were all anonymous. As for the name Sophia . . ."

"I received my name during Victorian times," said Sophia. She glanced lovingly over at Buckthorne. "What about him?" she asked. "Is he Jewish too?"

Michael George shook his head. "He is of Persian extraction," he said, "and according to Dr. Dieter Schmidt, first brought to the attention of Zerubabel by Zarathustra. Yet he, too, was without a name until the end of the Dark Ages, when the great Kabbalists designated the opposites of the heavenly host: Moloch, Oghiel, Belial, Beelzebub, the Dukes of Easu, Sathariel, Lucifuge, Azariel, Astaroth, Golub, Oriel, Asmodeus, Belphegor, Samael, and Lilith. Only Satan was known by name to the Scribes and the Prophets. As for where the label Buckthorne came from, I have no idea; Gilbert and Sullivan, perhaps."

"I took it for myself," said Buckthorne coldly. "From a rosebush and a goat, both of them symbols of temptation. However, from now on I should prefer to be called . . ."

He hesitated, while he tried out various names in his mind. Richard? Billy? John? H.R.?

"I think," he said at last, "I should like to be called Lancelot."

"Oh, lovely!" cried Sophia. "Absolutely smashing. Can you ride a horse?"

"No," said Buckthorne; "though I can ride the wind. Not, of course, the whirlwind, or a hurricane, but something under gale force: say, a good, steady forty-five knots. Not," he remarked, "that there'll be much time for riding, anyway." And he added glumly,

"I'll soon be back tending the fires again."

Sophia shuddered. "Please," she said, "have you no feeling for me at all? For what I'm going through?"

"Forgive me, love," said Buckthorne tenderly. And he added miserably,

"We have so little time! And we've already wasted most of it."

Turning to Michael George, he inquired,

"Is there some place where we can be alone?"

"There is a small room behind the kitchen," replied Michael, "where I used to put my guests."

"Thank you," said Buckthorne; and to Sophia,

"Come."

Chapter

12

SHE LAY drowsily in Buckthorne's arms. Well, she said silently, aiming her thoughts heavenward, *You* put me into a woman's body, not I; I didn't ask for it.

Buckthorne lay on his side, gazing at her anxiously. He hoped she had not expected anything out of the ordinary, since he had been given only the usual human equipment; what he didn't know was that she had not expected anything at all. As for what she actually felt, she was uncertain; there had been a certain amount of pain, but also a great joy. So that, she thought, is earthly love; there is something to be said for it. She felt an extraordinary tenderness for Buckthorne, not at all like that which she was accustomed to feeling for the cherubim who had been her lifelong companions until now.

"Just think," Sophia murmured, "I might have gone all through eternity, and never have known."

She thought of the night ride along the river, the dark arch of sky and the hovering stars, the gentle motion of the carriage, the steady clop-clop . . . "You said you would teach me someday," she said, blushing a little. "Tell me; have I had a . . . you know; whatever it is . . .?"

"Yes, my darling," said Buckthorne.

"That's good," said Sophia, nestling contentedly in his arms. She closed her eyes for a moment, and opened them to stare dreamily at the wall, papered in a faded pattern of cabbage roses and green leaves. There would be aphids on the roses, she thought; little insect things. Little, tiny . . .

"Microbes," she said suddenly. "I remember. We'd been talking about microbes."

Buckthorne nodded absently. "Microbes," he said. His thoughts were elsewhere. But all at once he stirred; and with a startled look, raised himself on an elbow, and stared down at her. "Microbes," he said; "a virus. Yes."

He drew a long, trembling breath. "It could be," he said.

"What could be, my love?" asked Sophia drowsily.

"The cause," said Buckthorne. "The cause of every-thing."

Sophia came awake suddenly. "Of course," she cried. "Oh, do you think so?"

Buckthorne dropped back again, with a helpless gesture. "Even if I thought so," he said, "what good would it do? Even if it were true, how could I ever prove it?"

"Would it be possible to get hold of a microbe," asked Sophia innocently, "and see what it looks like?"

"Isolate it?" said Buckthorne slowly. "Yes. One could do that. I hadn't thought of it. And then . . ."

"And then?" asked Sophia eagerly.

Buckthorne looked at her reprovingly. "I thought you weren't a scientist," he said.

"But I'm not," she insisted. "I don't even know what 'isolate' means."

The smile that Buckthorne gave her was almost boyish. "It doesn't matter," he said, taking her into his arms. "The thing is . . . you've given me an idea . . ."

Sophia's eyes widened. "You mean," she said, gazing at him in wonder, "that we're going to . . . you know . . . again?"

"There's just time," said Buckthorne.

Michael George sat by the window in the little kitchen, watching the road, the woods, and the cemetery, over which the shadows had begun to gather. Already the air was misty with the approach of evening. From the old orthophonic record-changer in the next room, he could hear the music from the second act of *Tristan und Isolde*. "*Habet Acht*," sang Brangaene, "*habet Acht!*"

The first assault was a terrific peal of thunder which all but blasted Michael's eardrums, and brought Sophia and Buckthorne upright out of bed. A moment later, Michael saw an enormous dog bound out of the woods and head for the house; but suddenly, coming to the cemetery, the animal hesitated, and finally, after sniffing uncertainly about, he lay down, his huge head between his paws, and a look of melancholy crossed his face, puzzled and uneasy above those long-buried bones.

"That's Hugo," whispered Sophia, peering out of the

window. "He knows I'm here; but he cannot tear himself away from the cemetery. I think he'd be happier as a policeman."

"Will there be others besides Hugo?" asked Buckthorne fearfully.

"Undoubtedly," said Sophia.

A sound as of a vast sigh, made by the fluttering of great wings, passed over the house; and a stern voice, but at the same time one of singular sweetness, intoned,

"Sophia!"

Sophia went to Michael George and took both his hands in hers. "You have been good to us," she said; "and I, for one, owe you more than I can say. You are a dear man, and I cannot let you suffer any more on my account. I am going out to Them."

And turning to Buckthorne, she took him in her arms. "Good-bye, dear friend," she said; "dear love."

"No!" cried Buckthorne. "Wait!" And Michael George also tried to detain her. "I am an old man," he said, "and I shall die soon in any case. As a matter of fact, a thunderbolt would do very well, very much better than pneumonia or a lingering illness."

But Sophia refused to be moved. She had made up her mind to accept the consequences of her behavior. "Have I really committed such a sin?" she demanded. "I may have done; if so, I must pay for it. But you, my dear," she said to Buckthorne, "you can still escape."

At that moment an icy wind tore through the house, breaking windows, and slamming all three of them against the wall. "It is too late," said Buckthorne quietly. "Beelzebub has seen me. I recognize his style."

In the cemetery, Hugo, too, appeared to understand that something had gone wrong, and rising on his haunches, he let out a long, dismal howl. Within a moment, a fiery bolt flamed through the clear evening sky, which struck a bush outside the house, and set it on fire.

"They are really in earnest," said Sophia.

Buckthorne shook his head gloomily. "That was a mistake, I'm afraid," he said. "The burning bush will infuriate them all over again."

And he gazed despondently at Sophia, who remained calm and resigned, though pale.

Beelzebub lost no time: the house was shaken to its foundations, winds of enormous strength tore shingles from the roof and uprooted trees; the kitchen table rose to the ceiling, the stove belched smoke, Michael George was flung facedown on the floor, and the second act of *Tristan* cracked in two. Loud shrieks filled the air, while, in the cemetery, Hugo dashed madly here and there, snapping at phantoms.

Buckthorne sighed. "The usual paraphernalia," he remarked.

Suddenly, however, a fiery cross appeared in the sky, from which arrows appeared to dart toward earth in a golden shower.

"Of course!" cried Sophia happily; and pressing into Buckthorne's hands her own rosary with its small gold and ivory cross, she exclaimed,

"No demon will dare to touch you now!"

"Never believe it," replied Buckthorne, returning it to her, and explaining that the sight of the cross only angered Lucifer the more, because, like the burning bush, it was a sign of his own failure. "There is only one way," he declared, "to keep the Devil at bay."

He went on to remark that none of his own people could stand the odor of garlic. "Even I," he said, "have always found it offensive, though now, for some reason, I find it less so."

Michael George, picking himself up from the floor, peered warily out of the window. "The Hartsdale Fire Department is coming," he announced.

Chapter
13

FIRE CHIEF Fred Andersen was puzzled: no matter how much water he poured onto the bush, the flames wouldn't go out. Besides, there was a lot of wind, and howling in the air. "God damn Almighty," he said to his deputy, "it's a clear night, and there's all this going on. I'm going to send to Scarsdale for help."

In addition, he decided to alert the chief of police in White Plains. "Look, Ed," he shouted over the field radiophone, "there's something going on down here that looks downright peculiar. There's some characters have got themselves barricaded in a house off Cemetery Road; I don't know how many they are, but they've got some sort of thing going out front like the Fourth of July, and I think maybe you'd ought to come down here and have a look."

The chief of police phoned the sheriff. "I'm going down to Harts Corners," he said. "Old Fred Andersen's got hisself some trouble, and I think maybe you'd better come along. I'm taking the FBI most-wanted list; seems there's a gang holed up there, might be that girl, what's-her-name, they're looking for; there's a horse and an old victoria tied up in the yard. You never know."

"We'll be there," said Sheriff Pitcher, and called his chief deputy.

In short order, then, fire trucks from Scarsdale, police from White Plains, and deputy sheriffs from as far away as Pleasantville converged onto the little cottage already under attack by forces even more awesome. Their blaring sirens only added to the din; the red, revolving top-lights of the police cars, the flashing searchlights of the fire engines, the streams of water crashing into the burning bush and against the walls of the house, the howling of the wind, the crackle of radiophones, the rush of unseen wings, the dreadful shrieks coming from somewhere in the air, all created a hubbub and a confusion beyond anyone's experience.

"Godalmighty," exclaimed Sheriff Pitcher, "what's going on here?"

Policemen and deputy sheriffs, holding their guns ready, crouched behind their cars, or ran like bucketing shadows to more tactical positions—kneeling, closing in—only to be thrust back by unseen forces. Fire hoses, like great snakes, wound in and out between the wheels of cars and trucks; Fireman Dooley stumbled over one of them, and it opened its mouth, red as a pomegranate, and hissed at him.

"Holy Mother of God!" he screamed, and climbing up

onto the nearest hook-and-ladder, he collapsed. Huge, shadowy forms, seen for a moment in the flashing lights, and lost again, froze more than one policeman to the spot in terror; a deputy sheriff, aiming at what he took to be an elephant, nicked the ear of an innocent spectator who, along with several dozen others, had come to see what all the excitement was about. Rumors and expectations ran high; it's a terrorist gang, said a bystander; it's the Communists, said another. A woman whose husband's second cousin was a film cutter in Hollywood was convinced that it was just a film being shot.

"It's always like this," she said; "bang bang bang. That's the way they have to begin." She pointed to the burning bush. "See?" she said. "Special effects."

Meanwhile the great dog was leaping and snapping at shadows everywhere. "God damn it," cried Fire Chief Andersen, "get that hound out of here! Turn the hose on him!"

Sheriff Pitcher stood, legs apart, in front of the cottage. "You in there," he shouted through his bullhorn, "come out with your hands up. You've got thirty seconds; you got any requests, I'm here to listen. You also got the right to an attorney. Thirty seconds. One . . . two . . . three . . . four . . ."

The full force of the water caught Hugo in the side and rolled him over. He rose indignantly, no longer a dog but a puff of smoke which rapidly expanded into a thick cloud covering the entire scene. And while the firemen, the police, the deputies, and the spectators stumbled about in the fog, through which furious, flaming shapes whizzed like rockets, Hugo, drifting in through the window, spoke to Sophia. "Come, Sophia," he said.

For a moment he appeared once more as the friendly London bobby. "Come, luv," he said; and to Buckthorne, with a nod, "They won't see you, lad, so be off with you."

Buckthorne turned for the last time to Sophia. "It's you and I, Sophia," he said. "Remember that. Because together we'll find the answer, and not apart. I think I love you; and that is something new in the world, and very important. Good-bye."

And he was gone, out the back door. In front, the counting went on: fifteen . . . sixteen . . . seventeen . . .

Hugo cleared his throat. "Not a bad lad, that," he said. "Well, let's get on with it."

And turning back into a cloud, he led Sophia out through the flashing lights and huddled cars, ghostly in the fog. No one saw them go.

The police found Michael George in the smoke-filled kitchen, quietly writing in his journal. "Where are the others?" they demanded, keeping him covered with a .45 Magnum, three World War One rifles, and a sub-machine gun.

Michael George looked up in surprise. "What others?" he inquired.

He gazed out of the shattered window, at the rumbling fire trucks, the circle of police cars, and the milling crowds.

"My goodness," he said mildly. "I seem to have missed something. What's been going on?"

Chapter

14

ONE OF THE most notorious criminals in the country, with half a hundred killings to his credit, woke in his cell at the State Minimum Security Prison, after a restless night. Already convicted ten times over, he was awaiting the result of his seventeenth appeal based on a technicality in the law. "Some sonofabitching mosquito kept after me all night," he complained to the guard. "The bleeping bug musta got a pint of blood off'n me."

Buckthorne was in a hurry; he knew that he had only a little time left, that he must find a laboratory to which he could take his precious specimen, and a hematologist who could analyze it for him. "Though what I probably need," he said to Dr. Rosenbluth of the Mid-Town Clinic, whose address he had found in the telephone directory, "is a microbiologist." And he explained that he was looking for a very special microbe, or virus.

"Fortunately," said Dr. Rosenbluth, who had studied

tropical diseases in the Far East, "we are thoroughly
equipped here. Though I must tell you that to find a
virus . . ."

He shook his head doubtfully. "I will do the best I
can," he said, "but it may take a little time."

"The future of the entire human race depends upon
it," Buckthorne assured him.

While the doctor bent over his powerful microscopes,
Buckthorne paced to and fro, backward and forward,
occasionally peering out of the window at the street
seventeen stories below. He tried to sit down, but found
himself too nervous. "Oh, Sophia," he murmured, "where
are you?"

At twenty minutes before noon, a speckled pigeon
alighted on the windowsill, and cocked a pink eye at him.
"Buckthorne," it croaked.

Buckthorne recognized Golub, one of the followers of
the Dukes of Esau. "Look," he cried desperately, "I need
more time. Just a little more time. I tell you—I'm on to
something. Something big."

"In the last twenty-four hours," said the pigeon coldly,
"there have been seventy-eight muggings, sixty-two of
them fatal; 189 rapes, 132 of which ended in killings, 109
of them by stabbing; 697 aggravated assaults with serious
injuries to the victims, forty-eight shootings, and three
hair-pullings at Kitty's Female Bar and Café. And all this
in Manhattan alone. As for the rest of the country—here,
read this."

So saying, he held out a folded scrap of newsprint in

his beak, for Buckthorne's perusal. "The chief wants to talk to you," he said.

However, he lingered a moment longer, before taking off. "I hear you had yourself a little chick from you-know-where," he croaked. "Is it true?"

And when Buckthorne refused to reply, he let out an evil chuckle. "Isn't that something!" he exclaimed. "Oh, my! Oh, my! From Up There! Fancy that! Whew!"

"Go to hell!" said Buckthorne, moving menacingly toward the window.

"I'm going, I'm going," exclaimed the pigeon, and flew away.

Considerably disturbed, Buckthorne found a seat against the wall, and opening the scrap of newspaper, glanced at its contents. It proved to be a single column entitled "The Southland," from the *Los Angeles Times.*

> Either of two bullet wounds might have been fatal to Los Angeles Bureau of Music Coordinator Owen Brady, 51, who died Saturday after being pulled unconscious from his flaming car, which had crashed into a wall at 820 West Blvd., the coroner's office reported. A postmortem examination revealed a number of bullet wounds in Mr. Brady's body, and the autopsy report disclosed that either the one in his head or another in his chest might have caused death. Police said they have no clues to the murder. The coroner's office reported the shots had been fired from inside the car.

A Montebello youth was shot to death as he watched television in the bedroom of his home, authorities reported. The parents of Alexander Castillo, 18, were awakened by a single gunshot. They went into their son's bedroom to find he had been shot once in the right side of the head. Police said the assailant apparently opened a sliding glass door and fired at Castillo. Officers were trying to determine a motive for the crime.

An 8-year-old South Pasadena girl was killed when the swing set on which she was playing in the backyard of her home fell and crushed her. Police said Tammy L. Lindsey was playing on the swing with her brother Larry, 13, when the set toppled, throwing the boy clear and crushing the girl beneath the heavy crossbar. Police said the swing set had not been anchored to the ground.

A Monterey Park man was shot to death during an argument with another man at his home, police said. Police booked Virgil L. Kirby, 30, on suspicion of murder in the death of Henry A. Avila, 44. Officers were unable to determine the motive for the shooting.

A Coachella youth was fatally stabbed during a wedding reception at Our Lady of Soledad Recreation

Hall. Mike Garcia, 18, was found lying in the street outside the hall where about 150 persons were attending the reception, police said. He died 90 minutes later at an Indio Hospital. Police said they found only one witness who admitted seeing the victim slump to the street.

A man who committed suicide after allegedly killing one Portland, Oreg. policeman and wounding another was identified by the FBI as a Los Angeles man wanted for a 1971 murder in San Bernardino. Authorities said the suspect, Robert William Powell, 25, shot the Portland patrolman in the heart as he attempted to search Powell in connection with a robbery. Another officer was wounded. Powell then fled and shot himself in a house two blocks from where the patrolmen were shot, police said. He had been sought by San Bernardino County sheriff's deputies since December 1971, for the murder of Michael D. Shaw, 25, of Riverside, who was shot twice in the head and then left in a burning sleeping bag in the Mojave Desert.

There was also another item from the same source:

Two of the three young men convicted of these crimes were former mental patients—released to the community, some say, as a direct result of the state's cutback of services for the mentally ill.

Herbert Mullin had voluntarily entered mental hospitals five times and each time had been discharged, though his psychiatric examinations had revealed violent tendencies. Another of the killers, Edmund Emil Kemper, had been released from Atascadero and paroled by the California Youth Authority after killing his grandparents. He climaxed his year-long spree of killing by murdering his mother. Frazier was a former CYA inmate; his behavior had been noticeably bizarre for at least a year before he killed the Ohta family and the doctor's secretary.

Chapter

15

SOPHIA stood before Gabriel, who regarded her with a stern expression. "You know, of course, that you have disgraced yourself," he said. "Not only that, but the entire Host, the saints, the martyrs, and the Church Militant. I cannot imagine what you can possibly say in your defense, but I am prepared to listen. For instance: were there any extenuating circumstances?"

Sophia lifted her head and gazed proudly at the great archangel in his shining armor. "There was every reason in the world," she said. "I was in love."

"Was?" demanded Gabriel.

"Am," said Sophia.

"Dear me," said the archangel.

And he added coldly,

"That is impossible. For an angel, to love is natural, for love is itself the nature of our being. But for an angel to *be* in love—and with a creature of Satan—is preposterous."

"I thought so too, at first," said Sophia. "However, it was you who sent me on this errand—an errand which I neither understood, nor expected to enjoy."

"No one expected you to enjoy it," said Gabriel. "It was simply your duty."

He gave a sigh of exasperation. "You've put us to a lot of bother," he declared. "All that batting about in Hartsdale. As though we didn't have troubles enough here at home."

"I'm sorry about that," said Sophia. "If I had been able to act differently, I would have. But you did choose an awkward moment to send Hugo; you could have waited."

"Why?" demanded Gabriel. "After all, it wasn't the first time you'd been sent down there, and nothing ever went wrong before. I remember in particular, during the reign of Queen Victoria . . ."

"I went as a boy then," said Sophia, "and I learned about cricket and grouse-shooting. This time I went as a girl—a woman, actually—or at least what passed for a woman . . ."

"Well?" demanded Gabriel.

"And Buckthorne completed my education," said Sophia simply.

"Damnation!" exclaimed Gabriel, and spoke in tongues for a while. Sophia stood in front of him, calm, meek, but obstinate.

"The fact is," she said when Gabriel was through, "that —just possibly—I didn't altogether fail after all. Because of Buck. He said I'd put him onto something rather splendid.

"You see," she went on, "we found out that we were on the same mission, more or less. He had been sent to stop the slaughter; and I was sent to find out what was causing it. He had already discovered the mass orgasm . . ."

"The what?" cried Gabriel, turning pale. "Please!" he murmured. "Spare me. Merciful heavens!"

And he added sternly,

"We are sexless Beings; devils, demons, imps, and demiurges are not."

"Yes, sir," said Sophia obediently, and lowered her head. But a moment later, she raised it again. "Just the same . . . ," she began.

"I don't wish to hear any more about it," said Gabriel.

Sophia stood her ground. "In that event," she declared, "I wish to present my case before God."

Gabriel was obviously taken aback. "You mean the Lord?" he asked, glancing around anxiously.

"Of course," said Sophia. "Who else?"

"The Lord," said Gabriel uncomfortably, "is very busy. He sees no one. To tell you the truth," he added, dropping his voice, "I haven't seen Him myself for years."

"You mean to tell me that God is too busy to see His own?" exclaimed Sophia. "I am shocked. I realize that I am only a lesser angel, of Jewish extraction, but . . ."

"We all are," said Gabriel impatiently. "So all right: you've learned that much. Even the Queen of England claims her descent from David. Get on with it."

"Very well," said Sophia. "I demand to see my Creator."

"Oh," said Gabriel in relief, "you mean HIM: the Infinite, the Eternal Himself?"

"Yes," said Sophia. "Quite."

"I've never seen HIM at all," said Gabriel.

Sophia stared at the great archangel in astonishment. "But then," she said, puzzled, "if you haven't seen HIM, who has?"

"I don't know," Gabriel admitted candidly. "Perhaps the Lord. I asked Him once, but He didn't want to talk about it."

Sophia sat down. Suddenly she had a lot to think about. "Well, then," she said slowly, "if *we* have never seen HIM, probably Satan never has either."

"By George, I never thought of that," said Gabriel cheerfully. "But that doesn't mean," he added quickly, "that there isn't such a thing as Evil in the world."

"Yet," said Sophia thoughtfully, "if we are both equally a part of creation . . ."

"Equally?" asked Gabriel, affronted. "Who said anything about equally?"

"I didn't mean in the ecumenical sense," explained Sophia.

"Oh," said Gabriel. "Well—proceed."

"What I meant to say," Sophia went on, groping for words, "if we could only work together, instead of against each other . . ."

"Out of the question," said Gabriel abruptly. He continued in gentler tones,

"My child, for myself I have never ventured beyond the solar system; such things as quasars, black holes, exploding stars, frighten me. But I know that in the universe there is order; there has to be. In any system, there must be a rule of checks and balances."

He sat himself down in his shining armor next to Sophia, who was still wearing her long, full skirt, her lacy blouse with its puffed sleeves, and the straw bonnet tied with a blue ribbon. "Long ago," he said, "Lucifer tried to upset that balance. He wanted to share his powers with those of the Lord, and vice versa. The Lord, very sensibly, cast him down . . . just as He also very sensibly broke up the conspiracy of Babel, saying: 'Behold, the people is one, and they have all one language; and this they begin to do; and now nothing will be restrained from them, which they will have imagined to do. Go to, let us go down and confound their language, that they may not understand one another's speech.' "

Sophia thought of Adelaide, and the House of Beauty, of the incomprehensible mouthings of Jingle, of the comfort of Buckthorne's arms on the long river journey, of breakfast in the sun on the grass of Van Cortlandt Park. And she thought of Michael George, and the little house in Hartsdale. "I wonder," she said, sighing, "if that was, after all, a wise decision. Think of the lovely world it might have been, if all they had imagined to do . . ."

Gabriel shrugged his mighty shoulders. "My dear," he said. "I'm only an archangel. How should I know?"

Chapter
16

BUCKTHORNE stood once more before the Council. He held in his hand a small vial of blood, a number of glass smears secured by a rubber band, and a dozen photographs.

"What I have here," he declared, his voice trembling with excitement, "is a discovery of the greatest importance."

Lucifer, lolling back against a dun-colored cloud, regarded him skeptically through half-closed eyes. The fallen archangel, Prince of Darkness, was annoyed; he had ordered this junior officer to put an end to indiscriminate slaughter on earth, and the clown had brought back photographs!

"I understand that you enjoyed a brief peccadillo with a female from the opposition," he said coldly. "Was that a way to spend your time?"

"It was not a peccadillo," said Buckthorne.

"Sir?" suggested Lucifer.

"Sir!" agreed Buckthorne hastily. "And," he added, "I have the photographs to prove it."

"Please," said Lucifer wearily, "we have seen plenty of such photographs before. I'm sure there is nothing original about them; even the Japanese haven't developed any new positions in the last thousand years."

Buckthorne drew himself up to his full height, which was still some twelve feet short of Belial or even Beelzebub, who—themselves dwarfed by their master—towered above him like thunderclouds. "These pictures," he declared, "are such as you have never seen before. They are microphotographs of a virus."

And he displayed several pictures of what appeared to be a squidlike creature with staring eyes and long, hairy tentacles.

"Ugh," grunted Lucifer, studying the prints. "What an ugly beast! What is it?"

"It is the virus megas, b.r.," replied Buckthorne proudly. "It is the answer to your question as to how I spent my time on earth."

And with a slight show of embarrassment, he added, "I will admit it is not the only answer, but it is the most important one. The 'b,' " he explained, "is taken from my own name, and the 'r' from Doctor Rosenbluth, who isolated it.

"The megas virus itself is responsible for megalomania, which, in my opinion, is the cause of those conditions which you sent me to correct."

"Well, well," said Lucifer; "well, well." He gazed at

the photographs, and then at Buckthorne. "And what are we going to do with it?" he inquired.

"Why," said Buckthorne enthusiastically, "we are going to develop an antibody to it."

"I see," said Lucifer. "And how will we do that?"

"With all due respect . . . sir," said Buckthorne, "we'll set our own doctors onto it."

"Sure," said Belphegor, "why not? We've got plenty. Crippen, Mesmer, Albertus Magnus . . ."

Lucifer sighed. "The good ones," he said, "are all on the other side."

And counting off on his fingers, he named them: "Pasteur, Fleming, Lister, Harvey . . ."

"Harvey?" snapped Beelzebub. "Never heard of him. And we have all those Germans who worked in the camps . . ."

"I've no desire to add to Hitler's prestige," said Lucifer crossly. "As a matter of fact, I'm beginning to resent the way some of our junior officers have started to salute me. That obnoxious '*Sieg Heil!*' "

His expression lightened for a moment. "Megalomania," he mused; "yes, I can see that: it follows, in a way. You don't suppose we could use any of the SS people's blood . . .?"

He shook his head gloomily. "I had forgotten," he said. "They no longer have any blood."

"We can get all the blood we need from earth," said Buckthorne. "And as for doctors and virologists . . ."

"Gentlemen," he said, turning to the assembled Council,

"I happen to have a friend in Heaven. As a matter of fact, it was she who first put me on to my discovery. I love her."

"Love?" asked Belial, puzzled. "What on earth is that?"

"Exactly," said Buckthorne. "What on earth . . . It would take too long to explain it. Later, perhaps. In the meanwhile, I'm sure that if I could only reach her . . ."

"In Heaven?" cried Beelzebub. "That would be the day!"

"They'd blast you out of the skies," said Asmodeus. "Like they did us."

"Impossible," said Lucifer. "I'd rather not even think about it."

"I believe I know a way to get there," said Buckthorne. He went on with growing enthusiasm:

"Once I see her—once we are together again—I'm sure I can convince Them to lend us the use of a few Nobel Laureates. And with the help of others still alive . . ."

Lucifer sighed thoughtfully. "I don't suppose," he said wistfully, "while you're there, you could look about a bit? And perhaps find out just what $E = mc^2$ really means?"

"I'll do my best, sir," said Buckthorne bravely. And turning to go, he could not repress a cry:

"We shall be together again, Sophia!"

"This I have to see," laughed Lilith from her seat on the Council.

Lucifer roused himself suddenly. "By the way," he said, "what's all this nonsense about garlic?"

But Buckthorne was already on his way.

Chapter
17

HE FOUND Michael George where he had hoped to find him, seated on the coachman's box of his victoria opposite the Plaza. The old novelist was overjoyed to see him again. "Mr. Buckthorne!" he exclaimed. "I scarcely expected you to return. What a pleasure! And the young lady, Miss Sophia? I suppose I ought to say Ms., but I dislike doing so; it not only has an ugly sound, but fails to distinguish between youth and age, hope and disappointment."

However, when Buckthorne told him what was in his mind, his expression altered; his jaw sagged, and a look of disbelief appeared on his face. "Up there?" he asked, pointing to the sky. "My dear friend, you ask the impossible. Even in the old days such a thing was never suggested, not even by Scott and Zelda themselves."

"Nevertheless," said Buckthorne, "we'll make it. I promise you."

Michael shrugged resignedly, and gathered up his reins.

"Well," he said, "if you say so." And drawing his whip from its holder, he clucked to his horse. "Up you go, Maggie," he cried. "Not onward—upward!"

On the avenue, around the fountain in front of the Plaza, among the little hot-dog carts lining the entrance to the park, people stared at the sky in amazement. "It's a bird!" cried some, while others, later, described it as a winged chariot. "It's Elijah!" cried some in awe, and fell to their knees, or immersed themselves in the fountain already filled to capacity.

"Swing low, sweet chariot," sang several male members of the Glee Club from Howard University who had been visiting the city, while a group of young women from CCNY broke into "Ezekiel saw the wheel, High up in the middle of the air."

That evening the TV newscasters announced an unknown flying object sighted over Central Park, a sighting which the Air Force was unable to explain. The following day the *London Times* gave the incident a short paragraph in its section devoted to bird-watching, under the heading: AN UNUSUAL TAKE-OFF.

The *Los Angeles Times* failed to mention the event.

Sophia and Buckthorne exchanged a long and joyous embrace while Saint Peter looked away.

"I knew you'd come," exclaimed Sophia. "I hoped and prayed . . ."

It was Buckthorne's turn to place a warning finger on her lips. "My darling," he said, "let's not complicate things. I'm here to bring our two opposite hosts together. Of course," he added quickly, "to be with you, too; but first of all, we have work to do. Can you arrange a meeting for me with the Archangel Michael, do you think? Or Gabriel?"

"Gabriel is waiting for you, actually," said Sophia. "I've already explained everything."

"Everything?" asked Buckthorne.

"Well . . . nearly everything."

Buckthorne heaved a sigh of relief. "In that case," he said, turning back to Michael George, "we probably won't be needing you any longer." He hesitated for a moment. "Still," he said, "it might be better if you hung around for a bit, just to be sure."

"I should like that very much," said Michael George. "I shall have time to write a few lines."

And settling himself contentedly in the rear of the victoria, surrounded by clouds like flowers, he opened his journal.

Heaven, he wrote, is not at all what I expected. And yet —what did I expect? Ivory and gold? The gods of Greece lived for two thousand years on Olympus, a snow-capped mountain often lost in clouds like these. And before them, there was An, the heaven-god; Nammu, goddess of the primeval sea; Enlil, the god of air; Enki, of water; Utu, the sun god. They lived in the skies above Ur, above Erech, above the ziggurats of Babylon and other lost cities; gods or angels, they must all live somewhere. Only the Creator Himself lives nowhere and everywhere.

Hand in hand, Sophia and Buckthorne stood before Gabriel, while Michael and Raphael lounged in the background. "I understand," said Gabriel, "that you two have made an arrangement of some sort."

"Sir," replied Buckthorne, "Mighty Power, I come not only as a suitor for the hand of this one angel" (here he gave Sophia's hand a squeeze), "but as an emissary from my own people. We—that is Sophia and I—have made a fabulous discovery; and now what we need is the means of putting it to use for all our sakes."

And he described in detail his discovery of the virus megas b.r., the factor leading to megalomania. "What we need," he explained, "is to find an antibody which can be made into a serum, to be injected into men and women of all ages and conditions, white, brown, black, and yellow, thereby controlling the violence with which the world is afflicted, and which I believe to be the inevitable result of megalomania."

The three archangels agreed that Buckthorne's discovery was an important one, and that his project was interesting. "But will it work?" asked Raphael.

"Why not?" demanded the demon. "Humanity has already conquered yellow fever, smallpox, polio, the plague, measles, and diphtheria. Why not megalomania?"

The archangels looked at one another. Michael was the first to speak. "As the fellow says, why not?" he asked. And Gabriel, agreeing, remarked,

"What have we to lose?"

"Very well," said Gabriel finally. "Tell your master that

we agree to go along with the plan. But this affair between you and Sophia . . ." he added sternly.

"We need each other!" cried Buckthorne. He looked around him, at the clouds of heaven which hid the heavenly host. "No," he said, "no. It will do you no good to thunder—just as it will do us no good to loose our howling winds. Fear will get us nowhere; there is too much fear as it is. Only together can we hope to save mankind from suicide. And without mankind . . ."

He spread his hands helplessly. "What will become of us?"

"I know, I know," said Gabriel. "What do you want us to do?"

Buckthorne shook hands with the three archangels. "By the way," he said, as he and Sophia stepped into the victoria once more, "you wouldn't happen to have some simple explanation for $E = mc^2$, would you?"

"Frankly," said Gabriel, "I haven't the foggiest."

Chapter

18

THERE was indeed a great deal to be done, and Buck-thorne busied himself with setting up an organization. First of all, a considerable amount of blood had to be collected, distributed, and the virus megas b.r. isolated, extracted, and incubated in various cultures. The collection itself was left to the mosquitos and other blood-sucking insects such as ticks, bedbugs, and the tsetse fly, to vampire bats, and leeches. The subjects, or donors, were drawn from far and wide, from all quarters of the globe, with the exception of certain islands in the Fiji Basin and the Bismarck Archipelago. The best results were obtained from pop artists, rock singers, television producers, *auteurs,* best-selling novelists, politicians, literary critics, avant-garde poets, athletes, bureaucrats, African Chiefs of State, Jewish sculptors, and Russian Commissars.

The actual isolation of the virus megas b.r. presented no problems, a considerable number of foundations, universities, and clinics providing the necessary facilities. Once the technicians knew what they were looking for, the microscopically tiny cell was comparatively easy to spot.

But when it came to discovering an antibody, there were any number of embarrassing and unexpected difficulties. The search proved long, and discouraging. In the United States, men like Salk, Goode, Jenner, and Frank worked day and night, aided and comforted by suggestions from above, from such figures as Lister, Fleming, and Semmelweiss. (However, it was noted that the British scientists were more inclined to help their own compatriots than to share their knowledge with the Americans.) In Europe, on the other hand, work proceeded slowly; the French held back, uncertain how France could profit from the project to a greater degree than her neighbors, while the Germans were inclined to argue over the possibilities of Gestalt therapy and encounter groups, as opposed to inoculation. As for the Russians, they found the strange, squidlike creature with the untidy hair entirely natural, and altogether Russian.

During this period, Buckthorne and Sophia were often separated, encouraging their fellow workers in distant parts of the globe; and they were lonely for each other.

"My love," wrote Sophia from Alaska, "it is very cold here, but there are a lovely lot of mosquitos. I have had to discard my bonnet, and now I wear a splendid parka made of muskrat skins. I have sent off several large packages of blood to the Jaretzki Institute of Immunology in Barchester, but it may prove unrewarding, since the Eskimo, for the most part, seems to be of a gentle nature, unassuming, and inured to hardship. I miss you very much. Keep well, and God bless.

Your Sophia."

Buckthorne, who received this letter in Ankara, was for a time too busy to answer it; the supply of blood from the Turks held such a high concentration of megas b.r., it kept several laboratories working day and night for weeks on end. When he did write, Sophia was in Mexico.

"My darling," he wrote, "I have come upon a disturbing fact: it is that the population of the earth, despite wars, famine, plague, murder, and every atrocity known to nature and man, is increasing at such a rate that already millions die every year of starvation, and that in two hundred years there will not be food enough for even a remnant. Perhaps, after all, we are only adding to the problem. Imagine my state of mind! What do you think?"

Sophia wired him to meet her at the Ritz in London.

Seated in the comfortable elegance of the restaurant, looking out on the quiet garden, they held hands and gazed into each other's eyes filled with joy, longing, and regret.

"My dearest," said Sophia, "what will come, will come. It is true that the population explosion, unchecked, will ultimately wipe out life on earth, even that of insects, without the opportunity of re-creating itself from the primordial soup due to the loss of the l factor. But just the same, we must press on, because we are attempting the only thing possible—to give mankind one less immediate enemy, himself, and thereby give him the chance to use his brains.

"Perhaps, with megalomania relegated to the past, along

with the black death, vapors, and the gout, men will find a
way to deal with their other problems in time to save
themselves."

The longing in Buckthorne's eyes turned to wonder.
"My dear," he said, "wherever did you learn all that? The
primordial soup, the l factor . . .?"

He was relieved to see that she still blushed easily. "Oh,"
she said casually, "I was able to do a little reading now
and then . . . scientific journals and things." She gazed at
him candidly. "You see," she said, "when I had to admit
that I'd had no scientific education, I felt . . . well . . . you
know . . . a little ashamed. So I tried to bring myself up to
date. I confess, I don't understand very much of it; you've
no idea how much there is to learn, so many new theories,
one after another. For instance, did you know that in 180
million years, the sun . . . or was it the earth . . .?"

She stopped in confusion. "I've forgotten exactly what
was going to happen, but it was something quite horrid."

"For myself," declared Buckthorne, gazing at her ador-
ingly, "I'd settle for a few thousand."

"Me too," admitted Sophia, turning pinker than ever.

Buckthorne toyed for a moment with his fork, but
noting Sophia's expression, put it down and picked up a
spoon instead. "I was thinking," he said slowly, "when this
is all over . . ."

"Yes?" she asked, her breath coming a little faster.

"Well . . . I mean . . . Damn it, Sophia," he burst out,
"we just *have* to be together! I mean—we can't go on like
this, meeting once every century or so—"

She nodded, her eyes on his. "Go on," she said.

"We must live together," he declared. "We must find a place, and move in together. I want to wake up in the morning and find you there. I want to go to sleep at night with you beside me."

"I want that too," she said quietly. "But who would marry us?"

He stared at her in surprise. "Marry us?" he said uneasily. "I meant . . . what I meant was . . ."

"You didn't mean marriage?" she asked. "You meant just—what do they call it?—living together?"

"No, no," he exclaimed desperately, "I meant more than that. I love you. I can't imagine life without you. But . . ."

"But marriage?" she said coldly.

"After all," he insisted, "that's something of its own, isn't it? I don't even know if I'm ready for it. Responsibilities . . . I'd feel tied down. Besides—'they neither marry nor are given in marriage, but are as the angels . . .' "

"That's for the resurrected," said Sophia calmly. "Matthew 22:30. It has nothing to do with us. And as for feeling tied down . . .

"You'd feel secure," said Sophia. "And so," she added simply, "would I."

It was her turn to fiddle with cutlery. "But of course," she said, "if you don't want to . . ."

They sat staring miserably at each other. "Sophia!" he whispered.

"No," she said at last. "You see, my love, my poor love . . . if we simply lived together, we'd have the worst, not the best, of both hereafters. You'd feel responsible—and so would I; but neither of us would ever know just how responsible the other felt. We'd have made no promises to each other—taken no vows. And neither of us could ever give in, compromise, act unselfishly—not knowing how the other would take it, whether he mightn't think it an admission of weakness, of a need greater than his own. And earth would change under us, the sun would grow cold, our own end in sight at last—and still we'd be no closer to each other, not growing old together, but always apart, each in his single shell, you in yours, I in mine . . .

"Marriage is oneness: good and evil together in a singular comfort, wedded one to the other, like creation itself."

Swept by a powerful emotion which he did not understand, Buckthorne bowed his head. "Now praise we all our God," he whispered. "Here and hereafter. Demon and saint."

Sophia smiled happily. "Devil take us both!" she exclaimed. "Our dinner's getting cold!"

Chapter
19

THE BREAKTHROUGH was made at the Jaretzki Institute Laboratories in Barchester, where a team of virologists and immunologists working with Doctors Weaver, Walker, and Wibberley discovered in one of the samples sent to them from Sophia in Alaska, an antibody so small that only the strongest electron microscope could trace its course, and only by that detect its actual presence. It was, in fact, so humble a creature that they named it simply O, a variable having zero as a limit. Later, this was changed; and it became known as s alka j w^3—for Sophia, Alaska, the laboratory, and the three doctors.

But for a long while it eluded them. It was five months before they were able to capture its actual image; it took another six months to isolate it, and two years to form a culture in which it could be grown, cultivated, taught to divide, and turned into a serum.

The first experiment was a failure. It was injected into a

shrew, but the little animal remained as fierce as before. And the second experiment, performed on an orangutan, was only partially successful.

It became apparent that megalomania was a disease affecting humans rather than animals.

The first experiment on a human being was performed in the death row of San Quentin Prison in California. It had to be carried out with the utmost secrecy, due to the vigilance of the ACLU which had already obtained an injunction against any interference with the condemned man's civil rights. It was a complete success.

When this news was brought to Lucifer, he gazed around him with delight, cracked his knuckles, and crowed exultantly,

"I think he's got it!"

But it was another five years before s alka j w³ was accepted by the American Medical Association.

Meanwhile, an uneasy truce prevailed in the heavens, where the preparations for the wedding of Buckthorne and Sophia were slowly taking shape. There was no hurry, for it was felt that there was all the time in the world; and in fact, where day and night were one, and seasons passed without notice, time did indeed appear to stand still. On the one side, choirs of cherubim under Saint Cecilia were being coached in appropriate anthems, such as that of William Boyce for the wedding of George the Third, "Souls of Righteousness," Mendelssohn's Wedding March to *A Midsummer Night's Dream,* "Hail the bridegroom, Hail the bride" from *Ruddigore,* and a special cantata by

Johann Sebastian Bach, for soprano and alto, *Vergnügten Pleissen Stadt*. In his kitchens, Saint Lawrence and his cooks labored over a huge wedding cake composed of rose hips, cinnamon, pineapple, butternut flour, and marizipan, as well as an enormous trifle; Saint Anne put her seamstresses to work on Sophia's wedding gown, and Saint Valentine set about designing the decorations.

On the opposite side, the Dukes of Esau ordered vast cauldrons of hyssop and vats of spiced wine to be prepared, along with mountains of poppy-seed cakes for the assembled company. Belial, Beelzebub, Asmodeus, and the other high-ranking demons all ordered new robes, and fresh varnish for their wings; while Lilith gathered together all the perfumes of the Orient, salves and pomades, and commissioned Galanos to provide her with a gown of midnight-blue peau-de-soie, split up the middle.

And so the day itself finally arrived, and the two Hosts took up their positions on either side of the firmament, the family of the bride on the right, of the groom on the left, both the dark and the light shining like the sun. Sophia, on the arm of the Archangel Michael himself, stepped down from a cloud, her bridal train upheld by two Raphaelite cherubs, and followed by her maid of honor, Adelaide, whom she had brought up from Fifth Avenue for the occasion. Buckthorne, arriving in Michael George's carriage, was suitably attired in a pearl-gray cutaway, with top hat and gloves to match; he was accompanied by the old coachman in a faded Prince Albert, who had agreed to be his best man.

"Well, now," said Saint Patrick to Saint Teresa of

Avila, "what a fine day it is, surely: peace in Heaven at last; and a great example to Ireland, to say nothing of the rest of the world."

"Yes indeed," murmured Saint Teresa; but she remained pensive. "There are always the Jews," she remarked discontentedly.

"Ah, let the poor creatures be," said Saint Patrick. "God chose them Himself, didn't He now?"

Saint Teresa sighed. "There is no doubt that he chose them," she admitted, "but does He love them?"

"Not necessarily," said Saint Patrick. "Not necessarily at all."

Before an altar of spring flowers and under a canopy of roses, Buckthorne and Sophia repeated the age-old vows, drank the wine, and were officially married by the Arch-angel Gabriel in full regalia.

"Almighty Power," he prayed, "Who hath neither a Beginning nor an End, Who created the Hosts of Heaven and of Hell, and the Hosts before them, and before those Hosts yet other Hosts; Power in Whose Love none can be either greater nor less, gaze down upon us all, and upon these two of Your creatures whom I as Your priest have joined in holy matrimony. And if it be Your wish to bless them, bless them, for they are only doing what they believe to be Your will."

Buckthorne bent to kiss his bride; a great cheer went up, toasts were drunk, and dancing followed. A young demon attempted to pinch the bottom of a plump cherub, but received a bite on the fingers from Hugo for his pains. On the other hand, the hyssop made itself felt, as did the spiced wine and the sherry in the trifle; and presently everyone was dancing with everyone else, Golub with Saint Anne, and Lilith with the Seraph Azrael.

In the general confused hilarity, Buckthorne and Sophia escaped in the carriage, first throwing out the bride's bouquet which was caught by Adelaide; and went to spend their honeymoon in Hartsdale, at Michael George's little cottage. And the Pope excommunicated Gabriel for his part in the proceedings, an act which aroused a certain amount of discussion in the Church.

"Frankly," said the Jesuit Father Toner, speaking for himself, "I don't see how His Holiness can very well excommunicate an archangel; for either the Church created the angels, or they created the Church; I'm not exactly sure which, but either way the situation is anomalous, to say the least."

Chapter

20

BUT WHEN it came to making use of the serum, difficulties arose. The attempt to inoculate over four billion human beings of all ages and conditions soon proved itself to be impossible, if only for lack of facilities; there were simply not enough hospitals, clinics, laboratories, doctors, technicians, or public nurses for the task.

And there were other difficulties. The Russians, needless to say, had no desire to change their manners; and other nations also held back. In China, the serum was denounced as an attempt by Western capitalism to subvert the teachings of Mao; in Africa s alka j w³ was believed to be the secret juju of American imperialism.

It was Sophia, aided by her husband, who solved the problem by drafting all the stinging insects into Operation Humanity. "Instead of venom," she explained, "you will inject our serum into every human being, except the Aborigine."

It is to be understood that this produced some anxiety among the wasps, bees, spiders, centipedes, scorpions, and hornets. "Without our venom," complained the latter, "we shall all be the victims of the bloodsuckers, the horsefly, the ladybug, and the mosquito.

"Besides, what is there in it for us?"

"Without man," Sophia replied, "you would soon multiply to such an extent as to upset the balance of nature, with the result that you would soon perish from sheer weight of numbers. As for the bloodsuckers, they are exhausted from their labors, and I am sure they will be glad of a rest."

She did, however, exempt the egg-laying Eumenidae, out of respect for motherhood.

Of course, it didn't happen all at once; the inoculations took time. But within six months, it was possible to walk the streets of New York and San Francisco during the daylight hours without fear; and four months later, even at night. And people greeted one another with smiles.

The old novelist closed his journal with a sigh. It was all done; it had been fun writing it, but it was finished. However, after a moment he opened it again, and crossed out the last line. "No," he said, shaking his head; "that's going too far altogether. No one would believe it."

And he closed the journal once more, and laid it away in his desk. "But wouldn't it be wonderful," he said, "if they did!"

"Wouldn't it?"

Books by Robert Nathan

NOVELS

1951 *The Innocent Eve*
1950 *The Married Look*
1950 *The Adventures of Tapiola*
       containing *Journey of Tapiola, 1938*
       and *Tapiola's Brave Regiment, 1941*
1949 *The River Journey*
1948 *Long After Summer*
1947 *Mr. Whittle and the Morning Star*
1943 *But Gently Day*
1942 *The Sea-Gull Cry*
1941 *They Went on Together*
1940 *Portrait of Jennie*
1938 *Winter in April*
1938 *The Barly Fields*
       containing *The Fiddler in Barly, 1926*
       The Woodcutter's House, 1927
       The Bishop's Wife, 1928
       The Orchid, 1931
       and *There is Another Heaven, 1929*
1936 *The Enchanted Voyage*
1935 *Road of Ages*
1933 *One More Spring*
1925 *Jonah*

POEMS

1962 *The Married Man*
1950 *The Green Leaf*
1945 *The Darkening Meadows*

1944 *Morning in Iowa*
1941 *Dunkirk*
1940 *A Winter Tide*
1935 *Selected Poems*

THEATER

1966 *Juliet in Mantua*
1953 *Jezebel's Husband & The Sleeping Beauty*

FOR YOUNG PEOPLE

1968 *Tappy*
1959 *The Snowflake and the Starfish*

ARCHAEOLOGY

1960 *The Weans*